# UNSEEN CONSEQUENCES

HEATHER MICHELLE

# Books by Heather Michelle

IN RECOMMENDED READING ORDER

## The Misplaced Children Series

A Misplaced Child

A Misplaced Hope

A Misplaced Life

## Novellas

Forever Misplaced

Unseen Consequences (you are here)

## The Unseen Series

A Girl Unseen (Coming 2023)

*This is a work of fiction. Names, characters, places, and incidents either are the product of the author's imagination or are used fictitiously.*



Late for Dinner Press LLC
P.O. Box 982
Acworth, GA 30101



Edited by Nicole Schuette: www.nicoleschuette.com

*First Edition: October 2022*
ISBN 978-1-952857-14-0

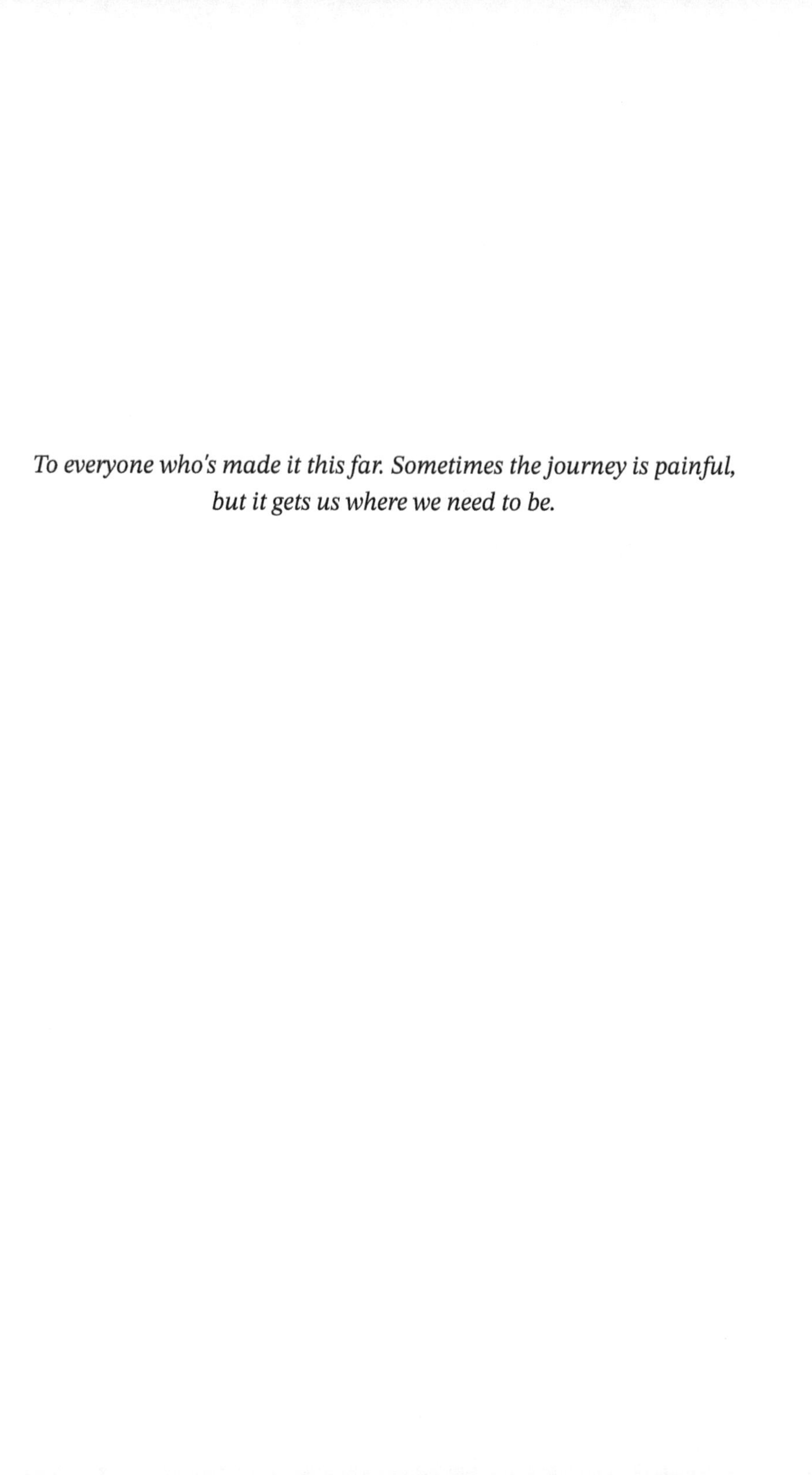

*To everyone who's made it this far. Sometimes the journey is painful, but it gets us where we need to be.*

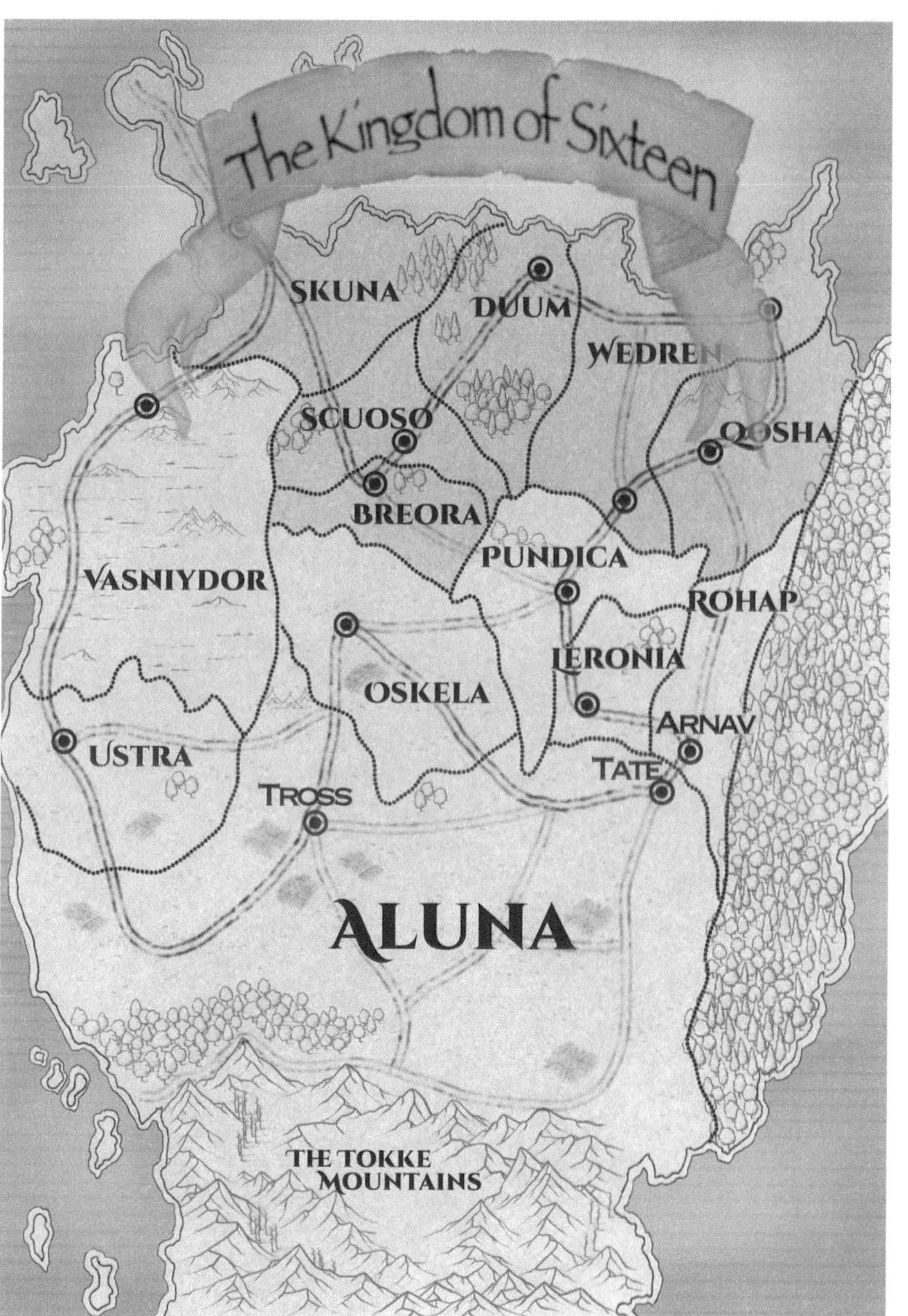
The Kingdom of Sixteen
SKUNA
DUUM
WEDREN
SCUOSO
QOSHA
BREORA
PUNDICA
VASNIYDOR
ROHAP
LERONIA
OSKELA
ARNAV
USTRA
TATE
TROSS
ALUNA
THE TOKKE
MOUNTAINS

# Unseen Consequences

AN UNSEEN NOVELLA

HEATHER MICHELLE

# Chapter One

"Never in my life have I been so insulted," Sword Master Cavall said as he flung open the doors of the king and queen's private sitting room.

Kamron sighed and followed down the hall on light feet. He leaned against the sitting room's doorjamb, just out of sight, as Cavall stormed into teatime. This was the problem with an informal king and queen who refused to stand on ceremony. It meant every time Kamron frustrated his tutors or offended some lord, they felt no qualms about interrupting the king and queen, no matter where they were or what they were doing.

It was quite inconvenient.

King Silas and Queen Elodie of Aluna, the largest and most supreme country on the continent, sighed in unison and set down their tea as the sword master stomped over the antique throw rug.

"Too far. The boy has gone too far. Peppering me with insults for weeks. I was in the guard for twenty years, you know. I can take my fair share of mockery. I should be able to manage a ten-year-old," Sword Master Cavall said.

"Cavall, welcome," King Silas greeted.

"Can I pour you some tea?" Queen Elodie asked.

Cavall ignored the queen and turned to the king, shaking his finger. "He acts all innocent, you see. Then he says little things that grate on you, like my wife making potato pie." He made a grinding motion with his hands.

"But what did he say, Cavall?" Queen Elodie asked. A curl of her graying-brown hair fell into her face and she brushed it away as she targeted Cavall with her piercing blue eyes filled with artificial sympathy. She dropped an extra lump of sugar in his tea.

Cavall looked down at the queen in her seated position, and his face grew purple. He blew out a breath and sputtered before shaking his head. "The words are of little importance, my lady. The point is the little monster must be taken under hand before he is ruined for any noble trade."

King Silas frowned and stood from his seat, towering over Cavall. "Now Cavall, I know you are frustrated, but remember yourself before you say something you will regret."

Cavall's head snapped up and he looked at the king, as he shuffled back a step. Kamron covered his mouth to stifle a laugh. It was a beginner's mistake insulting someone in front of the king.

"Beg your forgiveness, Your Majesties." Cavall looked as if he wanted to say something else, but the color in his face faded, and he took another step back, and bowed. "I regret to inform you I am retiring my post effective immediately. Enjoy your tea."

Cavall turned on his heels and exited the sitting room faster than he had entered. Kamron ducked into the shadows, a little victory chime ringing in his mind. Getting rid of Cavall hadn't been so hard.

The queen let out a deep breath from within the room, but before Kamron glanced back to see her mood, the king spoke, his voice firm and demanding. "Kamron, come here, please."

Kamron's stomach fell. How did they always know when he was listening? His victory feeling shallow, Kamron trudged into the sitting room. "Yes, Father?"

"What did you say to your sword master?"

Kamron glanced up and wished he hadn't. The king's vivid emerald-green eyes, the same shade as his own, glared down. Though Kamron resembled his father, his complexion was several shades lighter than his father's coal black, a perfect mix with his mother's peachy white. Kamron held in a sigh. He hated the disappointed look almost as much as he hated the scolding one.

"I said a lot of things to him, he was my teacher."

"And what did you say that had the man so embarrassed he wouldn't look me in the eye when I've known him fifty years?"

Kamron sighed and looked at his feet. "I just said his sword wasn't as long as yours. I don't know why he got so mad."

His mom made a choking cough noise, which usually meant he wouldn't be getting in too much trouble, but when he spared a glance at his father, the disappointment had only shifted to scolding mad.

"Can you explain why you wanted your sword master to quit?" his father asked.

"I didn't *want* him to—"

"Spare me."

Kamron balled his fists. "Begging your pardon, sir. I didn't *want* him to quit. I just decided to see if I could make it happen." Kamron never *wanted* anything. He rubbed at the albatross-shaped birthmark on his forearm, twin to the mark on his mother's collarbone. To want was dangerous. He'd known ever since his mom explained their family curse. Instead, he put his mind to things purely for the satisfaction of seeing if he could make them happen. If the end result was to his benefit, that only made victory sweeter.

His dad rolled his eyes.

"And why did you decide to see him quit?" his mom asked.

"Because I didn't like him. And because Dad is a better swordsman."

King Silas let out a deep sigh, put his hands on his hips, and looked at the floor. Kamron knew his dad was trying not to laugh, and the victory chime rang again in his mind. His dad knew he was a better swordsman, he would surely give in and teach Kamron himself.

King Silas straightened and looked down at his son with a frown. "I may be a better swordsman, but what makes you think I would teach you?"

What? Of course dad would teach him. It was the most logical answer. He'd planned it all out, right down to the clever insults he delivered each sword practice until his teacher finally lost it. Cavall was a stickler for propriety. He knew it would work, and it did.

Kamron frowned. He didn't know what answer would work to sway his dad, so he went with honesty. "But you're the best swordsman in the kingdom, maybe in the whole Twoshy. Why wouldn't you teach me, Dad?"

"Because I have other tasks I must see to during the day, and teaching fledgling swordsmen has never been a strong gift of mine."

"But you spar with the squires and the first-year knights all the time."

"Yes," King Silas said with a firm jaw and single eyebrow raised. Kamron knew that look—this was a trap. "The squires and knights are already proficient swords people who can gain much from sparring with me. You, on the other hand, are still a beginner and would benefit much more from learning the basics at the hands of a talented teacher, like Cavall, who is one of the best *teachers* in the kingdom."

Kamron glanced at his mom, who sat sipping her tea with the little smile that meant she was enjoying her husband telling someone off. Kamron frowned, because he was the one being told off.

Silas continued. "But I suppose now I have to find the second-best teacher to continue your studies."

Kamron bit the inside of his cheek. This plan hadn't quite gone as he expected it, but that sometimes happened when his plans collided with his mother or father, who both seemed so much more aware of his tricks.

"Well, what about Sword Master Bing? He's better than stodgy old Cavall any day."

"Oh, Sword Master Bing who currently happens to be tutoring your best friend?" Queen Elodie asked before shooting a glance at the king.

Mom might be on to him, but that didn't mean she would say no. Kamron crossed three fingers behind his back for luck. His parents exchanged glances as if having a full-on conversation that Kamron couldn't read quite yet. They weren't arguing with each other. They agreed on a few points, but were arguing with themselves, maybe? He wasn't sure.

His mom closed her eyes and shook her head slightly while exhaling. That was a good one. It meant she was going to do something she didn't think she should do and that usually went in Kamron's favor.

The king turned back to his son. "Do you really want to spend your last free year before page training in Rohap instead of here with your mother and myself?"

Kamron clamped his lips together to prevent the resounding yes from spilling out. Instead, he went for his second answer.

"I think the experience would be good for me, don't you, Dad? Besides, you should just spend the year in Tate instead of Tross. It doesn't make any sense for the capital to be here instead of closer to our allies."

"Now, Kamron, how many times do I have to tell you, a capital can't just be packed up and moved. There are a lot more details and planning that go into it," his mom said.

"Right. So why not start that? You and Dad are amazing planners. I know, if you tried, you could totally make it work."

His parents shared a sigh.

"Enough of this." Silas sat down and picked up his teacup. The victory chimes cheered in Kamron's mind. "I will write a letter to King Corinne and ask if you can spend the summer with his son."

"Woooo!" Kamron cheered. It wasn't his original plan, but it was nearly better.

"Yes, my little Slytherin," his mother said, stroking his head. She grew up in an illusion created by an evil wizard, so she said weird things like that sometimes. "Now go on and stay out of trouble before we change our mind."

Kamron grinned and skipped from the room. He would write Lukas, his best friend and crown prince of Rohap, straight away. It would be the best summer ever.

As Kamron packed to spend the summer with Lukas, his parents packed, planning to leave the capital Tross in favor of their castle home in Tate, a blooming city in the east, only a half day's ride across the border to where Lukas and Kamron would be studying.

The two boys spent the hot sweaty months of summer building up their endurance, strength, and the skills needed for life as a page, not through laborious training, but through their competitive natures. They often crossed the border, the proper guards in tow, splitting time between their two families' castles.

If only his family were always in Tate, Kamron thought often. Then when he and Lukas were both kings, they could still see each other. The three- or four-week trip from Tross would make visits nearly impossible when they had responsibilities.

As summer ended, Kamron returned to Tross, and both boys entered page training in their respective countries. They worked hard to excel at their lessons so that when next they met, they could show the other up with all they learned.

It wasn't that Kamron *wanted* to be the best; he didn't let himself want for anything. The albatross on his forearm was a constant reminder, day after day, that every member of the royal line would have their life's greatest wants and desires end in ruin, and Kamron vowed not to follow the same fate. He instead worked to see what he could accomplish when he put his mind to it. Plain and simple logic.

# Chapter Two

"Gonna get me strung up in the stocks, he is," Bruno grumbled under his breath, loud enough for Kamron, only two paces away, to hear.

"I won't let them put you in the stocks, Bruno. You're my friend, okay?"

"I'm not your friend. I'm your servant. There's a difference."

"You can be both," the fifteen-year-old prince said, as he adjusted his tunic in the mirror.

While squires didn't usually have servants, Bruno had been assigned to Kamron since he was young, and it was only natural for him to fall back into his longtime routine when Kamron was in the castle. Bruno hated interacting with any noble, aside from Kamron, who he tolerated. He kept his rosy cheeks and big hazel eyes hidden behind his messy brown hair, and while Kamron wished the servant felt more comfortable in his own skin, he liked having him all to himself.

Bruno grumbled again, but this time Kamron couldn't make it out.

"Did I mention you're my favorite servant?" Kamron grinned, and held it until the man, older than Kamron by a few years, rolled his eyes. Kamron knew he won. But Bruno never made it quite so easy.

"If it's a bonfire you're wanting to build, why have me leave the oil outside the east servants' entrance?"

"It just seemed most convenient for you," Kamron lied. "Thank you for your help, Bruno. Take the rest of the day off and enjoy the city."

Bruno reached for the door. "I think a nice lounge in my room sounds like a better way to spend the day, thank you very much."

Kamron darted around the man and held the door closed. "Absolutely not. It's a holiday, Bruno. You must go out and enjoy the merriment. And don't come home until you've found someone to enjoy a dance with under the summer solstice sun. In fact, I order it."

Bruno gave him a look so dry it almost had Kamron reaching for his water glass.

"And if I haven't found merriment by sunrise, shall I be forever doomed to haunt the city streets, or may I be permitted to return to my room?"

Kamron sighed and opened the door, gesturing for the servant to exit. "If you are unsatisfied with the festivities by sundown, you may return to being the biggest grump in the castle."

"Gonna give me an ulcer," Bruno muttered and exited the prince's suite of rooms, his trademark slump deepening with each step.

"Happy Midsummer, Bruno!" Kamron called, closing the door slowly, so he might hear the servant's creative curses. Kamron smiled to himself as the servant's footsteps faded away. It would be a solstice for the history books, and with careful planning, it would be the start of something excellent.

Kamron cracked the door again and listened. When silence stretched past his patience, a small spark of excitement lit in his core. He rummaged through his bedside table for the key ring, then set off down the hall. He knocked on each door before opening it, or unlocking it, if needed, and proceeding inside, until he had checked every room.

As the capital of Aluna, the castle of Tross was enormous, but with its constant construction issues it had less inhabitable rooms than other castles in the country. The keep in Tate, his father's holdings, was larger and in much better condition than Tross, not that it was hard to be better than a city riddled with sinkholes and bad plumbing.

He opened a bathroom and slapped a hand over his nose at the stench of a full chamber pot. He bent in half, fighting against his turning stomach, but still checked the corners for someone living before closing the door and shaking off the odor. If this were Tate, every room would have proper magical plumbing with a private toilet and shower. Instead, Tross was three hundred years behind the magical advancements of the rest of the country.

Though a tedious task, Kamron didn't let his focus wander as he checked every room, closet, and cupboard from his floor up. He was used to menial tasks. Training to be a knight was no small feat, and his teachers seemed passionate about putting the young prince through his paces. Kamron didn't mind. He would be humbled as a squire, honored as a knight, and one day exalted as king. All part of his inevitable path, and while he would never want anything else, he always found ways to make that path more enjoyable. Like he was doing right at that moment.

After clearing the upper floors, Kamron crossed to the east wing and stepped down a few inches to the wooden platform that made up the continuation of the hall. A slight breeze escaped the cracks where the wood didn't meet the stone perfectly, and the temperature rose several degrees, lacking insulation from the warm summer sun. The floor creaked in places where it would soon need to be replaced, and the rugs and tapestries he passed were faded and worn.

He searched the wooden rooms from the top down. These rooms were smaller and closer together, making his progress slow.

He felt slight twinges of guilt as he unlocked and peeked into the servants' rooms, but it was all for the best.

All the rooms were empty, as they should be. The festival in front of the palace was well on its way, and a raffle would be held in forty-five minutes. The grand prize was a thousand gold pieces. Too high a purse for any of the crown's guests to pass up.

Kamron suggested all castle servants should be allowed to enter.

He didn't meet a soul on his journey until he made it to the fourth floor, where a sandy-haired squire with big blue eyes wearing the uniform of a neighboring kingdom unlocked a servant's room.

"Oi! Are we almost ready, then?" Kamron called.

Lukas grinned and stuck his head into a servant's room before relocking the door. "Just these few left."

Kamron nodded and divided the last six rooms with his best friend, checking each for occupants and meeting in the middle.

Kamron's nerves buzzed with anticipation. "Did you find anyone?"

"Just in the kitchens," Lukas said with a pointed look. "It's a small crew, and they all seemed disappointed to be missing the raffle."

Kamron let out a hard breath. "That's to be expected. Thoughts?"

Lukas ran a hand through his hair, mussing it in a way he seemed to favor lately. They hadn't seen each other in two years and it felt wrong for his best friend to have new gestures he didn't know. The two were inseparable, growing up. Tate and Arnav were only a half day's ride from each other, so whenever Kamron's parents grew tired of the conditions in the capital, they traveled to his father's ancestral home, and Kamron got to visit his friend. In their page days, the two best friends still got together over the summers, but at the age of thirteen, they became squires and were taken into service by knight masters, with no breaks or vacations in sight.

Kamron's knight master, a ferocious fighter, taskmaster, and commander of Aluna's Royal Forces, didn't believe in granting a squire a vacation just to see his best friend, and as Rohap was Aluna's closest ally, their duties kept them far from the northeastern border. As a highborn squire, Kamron was at the whim of his knight master until the day he would be knighted, usually at the age of eighteen or so. That meant another three years of service before he would see Lukas again.

Fortunately for Kamron, his knight master had duties in Aluna for the summer solstice that could not be avoided. Kamron spent three months before the holiday sending letters from his tent in a border camp in northwestern Aluna indirectly hinting and suggesting a delegation from Rohap should be invited to the celebration, and perhaps Sir Stonewall should be included. Sir Stonewall was knight master to the crown prince of Rohap, Squire Lukas, so it would be a worthwhile diplomatic journey all around.

It was hard. Tross was so far from Rohap making the journey difficult to justify, but a letter was sent about how the ambassador's son, a page in the capital, dearly missed her, and against all odds in their fifteenth summer, two squires, both future kings to their respective nations, found themselves once again in the same city. Both were even granted light duty by their knight masters as a holiday gift, with a promise of extra duties when the week was up.

They couldn't squander the opportunity, Kamron told Lukas, who vehemently disagreed at first. It took some explaining, but Lukas went along in the end, adding a few tweaks and suggestions to the plan, making it safer and more likely for success, as Lukas often did.

"The kitchens are on the west wing of the castle, ground floor," Lukas said, staring off down the hall as he thought. "It's charmed like crazy to prevent kitchen fires and is easy to vacate."

Kamron nodded. "Think we are set, then?" He wiggled his

fingers and a spark of blue flashed over the tips. He didn't have enough magic to warrant training, but he did have a knack for unraveling other magics—one of his favorite pastimes.

If Kamron couldn't get Lukas on board with a scheme, he gave up on it as a lost cause. Lukas nodded and held out his hand, where his own small blue spark flashed along his palm. Kamron clasped it and held for a beat before they stepped apart. A pact. They were in this together.

Decided, the two squires took off down the stairs to the east servants' entrance, where Bruno's supplies waited for them.

"It's too many," Lukas said as they looked over the sixteen heavy ceramic jugs filled with oil.

Sixteen had seemed symbolic, fated to success, when Kamron had made the plan, but the heavy ceramic jugs, tied together in twos with a length of rope to be carried over the shoulder, weren't as practical as he thought.

"What? Don't think you can carry it?" Kamron taunted. "Does Rohap not keep its squires in peak condition?"

Lukas crossed his arms and met Kamron's eyes. "Why don't you show me how it's done?"

Kamron found the first pair of jugs and hung them over his left shoulder, followed by a second pair. Then he found the ropes of two more pairs and lifted them with his other shoulder. There. Eight jugs each. He could handle eight. Kamron took a step, and his balance wavered. The jugs clinked together, and he set them down quickly.

"Two trips each, then?" he asked his friend brightly.

Lukas snorted and hung a pair of jugs from each shoulder. "First one to the top on their second trip wins?"

"Naturally," Kamron said, adjusting his burden until he too carried a more reasonable load.

They took off.

Kamron was first back to ground level to get his second load, but Lukas beat him back up by six steps. At the top of the eastern tower, both boys fell to the ground and lay gasping for several minutes. Kamron had spent the previous spring jogging in armor to work up his breath and strength, but he thought maybe he should move from hills to stairs. It was by far a harder workout.

Once his breathing was under control, Kamron lay on the floor a while longer, feeling the slight sway of the wooden tower in the breeze. It was an oddity in their world of strong stone fortresses for any part of a castle to be made of wood and quite an eyesore. It had been this way long before Kamron was born, when one of the many kings past had wanted to build Tross into the greatest castle in the Twoshy. Their family legacy, a curse passed down from generation to generation, spoiled the wants and desires of their royal line, and through its generational magic, opened one of the city's many sinkholes under the east wing of the castle. The temporary solution, which became much more permanent, was to rebuild in wood. They replaced the structure every few decades. It could get quite drafty, but they usually kept servants and guests they didn't particularly like in that wing, so it worked.

Kamron scratched at the albatross birthmark on his right forearm, proof of his bloodline, and the same curse running through his veins, and sat up.

"Shall we then?" Kamron asked, and the two set off to work on their plan, plugging the jugs of oil into an apparatus of wicks and fuses.

# Chapter Three

"Give me a moment, will you?" Lukas said.

They made it back to the festival with fifteen minutes to spare before the raffle. They joined a lively dance right off, to be seen and have a better excuse for their sweaty, disheveled appearances.

"Don't disappear," Kamron warned his friend as he left the dance. Lukas nodded and wove between the dancers into the crowd.

Kamron spotted his mother on the edge of the crowd speaking to a group of courtiers. She was lovely in a yellow linen that appeared simple and casual for the summer festivities but, on closer inspection, was covered in ornate embroidery of the finest quality. Simple elegance was his mother's style, and he admired it. Her dress's cut accentuated the birthmark on her collarbone, in the same way every shirt, tunic, and jacket he had ever worn had been cut to reveal the identical birthmark on his forearm. It made him stand out in a uniform that was supposed to give him anonymity among the squires, but as the head seamstress had always told him, that was the point.

Kamron waited until the dance moved him closer to the edge

of the crowd and caught his mother's eye. She shot him a look that said she knew he was up to something, before he grabbed her arm and pulled her into the dance. The queen laughed as her feet quickly found the beat.

"Where have you been?" she asked breathlessly, as Kamron turned her for a spin. She executed it perfectly, though her cheeks were growing red by the moment.

"Just looking for the loveliest dance partner at the festival. So glad I found you!"

His mom rolled her eyes. "Don't go wandering off again before the raffle. It was your idea, and you had better draw the lots yourself."

Kamron narrowed his eyes at her. "You just want everyone who loses to be mad at me and not you."

Queen Elodie grinned subtly, but did not reply as she spun once more. Kamron danced with her for a few more turns before calling a halt and leading her, red-faced and a little wobbly, to a chair. She grinned from ear to ear as she sat.

"Stay here while I fetch you a drink," Kamron told her, his eyes drifting to the castle before he navigated through the crowd. His parents were older than most of his peers' parents. They waited until later in life for him to arrive. When he'd grown old enough to realize this, he asked why they waited and why he didn't have any siblings. His mom had grown pale, and his father told him some questions didn't need asking. That was the end of it.

Once or twice, Kamron had thought to scheme his parents into giving him a sibling, but then he remembered his mother's pale face and the sadness in her eyes, and he let it go.

Kamron found a stall selling spiced cider and pulled out a coin when a heavy hand fell on his shoulder.

"There's my errant squire."

Kamron turned and came face-to-face with his knight master. Where once he'd looked up to her physically, over the last year he gained that extra two inches needed to rise above her smaller frame. The thought gave him a tiny point of pride. She could still beat the crap out of him in arm-to-arm combat, but with someone of her accomplishments that was expected. Her clear blue eyes sparkled as if she knew what he was thinking, and he silently hoped he wasn't about to be saddled with a task on his day off. He bowed respectfully. "Lady Knight, how may I be of service?"

"None of that," his knight master said, shoving him out of his bow. "If today is a holiday, I expect you to address me properly."

Kamron grinned. "Yes, Auntie Dess."

Lady Candescence of Lacanto, commander of the Alunan Royal Forces, councillor to the king and queen, cackled, and pinched his cheek. She wasn't his aunt by blood, but that rarely mattered.

Kamron pulled out another coin and bought Dess a cider. "This one is for my mother," Kamron explained, holding up the spare.

"I'll join you. I need to speak with her." She took the cider and flicked her long golden braid over her shoulder before sipping her drink.

Kamron led the way through the crowd, his eyes lifting briefly to the castle. The party was being held on the empty stretch between the front steps of the castle and the first wall leading down into the city. It was the largest open space in all of Tross that didn't have any inconvenient sinkholes. Revelers falling into bottomless pits tended to ruin the mood.

He turned to his knight master. "Are you making merry for the solstice?"

"No. Too many politics for my taste."

Kamron nodded. Dess was an old family friend of his parents, and her dislike of politics was legendary and the catalyst that made her pick up her sword and return to the field after her youngest went off to the magical university. As the commander of the Royal Forces, her duties should have kept her in the capital or at least more central than a border camp, but Dess insisted with tensions rising between Vasniydor, Aluna's northeastern neighbor, and the rest of the continent, commonly known as the Twoshy, it made more sense for her to stay close, help in training new recruits, and keep a pulse on the coming conflict.

Kamron knew it was an excuse to avoid council meetings, but he enjoyed life in the border camp. If only it wasn't so boring.

His mother was not where he'd left her. She was a short distance away in another dance, this time with a much taller partner. Kamron sighed. Would he ever be as tall as dad? A monolith of a man, even in his older age.

Shooting a glance at the castle once more, he froze for a moment. Was that smoke? Hard to tell in the overcast sky, but it was still a bit early.

Kamron's eyes found another familiar figure dancing in the crowd. Lukas dipped Iris, Kamron's second cousin, and spun her like an expert. Iris's dark face glowed with a red blush that made her beautiful. Kamron narrowed his eyes. He hoped his best friend and cousin weren't setting their sights on each other. He would have to say something. His best friend longed for a love match to rival the epic tales, but he was only fifteen, for the gods' sake. There was plenty of time for that.

The song ended, and the king dipped the queen in a romantic swoop. The crowd cheered and Kamron groaned. He didn't get the appeal of a love match. Why would he ever pick someone who would be a weakness in his armor? Didn't his mother see the danger?

His eyes rose to the castle again. He couldn't see the eastern tower from here, but perhaps some of the wispy white he saw in the muddled overcast was smoke.

As the dance broke up, Kamron weaved through the revelers and reached his cousin's side just as Lukas lifted her hand. To kiss it or bow over it? Yuck. Kamron gave them a sappy smile and clapped. "Brilliant, Lukas. I'm glad to see your training hasn't prevented you from getting so skilled in the dancing arts. You must be quite popular with *all* the ladies." Lukas looked at him blankly, and Kamron switched his gaze to his cousin who frowned at her shoes. “Iris, lovely to see you made it from Tate. Are you enjoying all the city has to offer?”

Iris looked up and glared at him, her blush a deep ruddy color. “Not anymore, dumpling.” She turned and disappeared into the crowd.

Kamron grimaced at the nickname her mother used when he was a toddler. “It’s a pain when they’ve known you since you were small and soft, isn’t it?” Kamron asked.

“Whatever,” Lukas said, brushing past him.

“What? You aren’t really mad, are you?”

Lukas paused, his face screwed up with anger. “That wasn’t cool.”

“Oh, come on. You can’t tell me you’re actually interested in my cousin? The one who used to chase us with sticks and insist we duel her?”

“She also won half the time, if you’ve forgotten.”

“We were seven!”

“And she was six.”

Kamron rolled his eyes and Lukas kept walking, pushing through the crowd until they reached the stage where the raffle would be held. The stage faced west, so the castle would be behind them. Kamron itched to turn and look, but he did not. “Look. All I’m saying is you shouldn’t settle on the first girl who can beat you with a stick.”

Lukas grabbed the basket of short sticks they would use to draw lots and brought it to a long table where a guard stood watching over the prizes on display for all to see. “What’s done is done. Just leave it alone.”

Kamron sighed and helped his best friend feed all the sticks into the large spinning basket, often used in betting games, that would shuffle the small, numbered sticks. Lukas would get over the event. And if he didn’t, Kamron would apologize and it would be forgotten.

According to the clock tower, there was still another five minutes before the raffle would begin. Kamron nodded to Lukas who made three small balls of blue magic and shot them one after the other into the air over the raffle table where they exploded into a shower of sparks.

Slowly, the crowd of revelers made their way to the stage, pointing and debating the value of the different prizes on the table. There was no doubt that the grand prize was the best, but they discussed if the gold hairpins or the year's supply of roast from the butcher was a better value. The satchel of tea closest to Kamron shouldn't be considered valuable at all, but the blend was one his mother had made that treated several aches and ailments and tasted delicious.

With two minutes to go, the king and queen made their way onto the platform. "Are we ready?" the king asked Kamron.

"We've been ready all afternoon, Yer Majesty," a woman Kamron recognized from the kitchens answered. A few chuckles and yelled agreements rang out.

King Silas found the woman in the crowd and shot her a grin. "Thank you, Anni. I'm glad to hear it. Tell me, what are you hoping to win today?"

Anni didn't hesitate. "The grand prize, after all."

King Silas nodded. "A noble pursuit, to be sure. And what would you do with such a bounty?"

Anni, the kitchen maid, shot a grin to her neighbor in the crowd and turned back to the king. "I definitely wouldn't be thinkin' of giving notice, Yer Majesty." She bowed to the king, and the queen snorted.

"Glad to hear it. We would miss your turnovers in the castle," Queen Elodie replied.

Kamron itched to turn and look at the castle.

Silas turned to him and nodded. "Shall we?"

Kamron cleared his throat and stepped forward. "Thank you all for attending this celebration of the solstice. Now I won't keep you waiting any longer. Once the raffle is over, the proper celebration can begin." A light cheer went up and Kamron waited for it to die before continuing. "Now everyone should know how this works, but let's recap. Each of you have a stick with a number"—several people waved their sticks in the air—"and a corresponding stick lives in this basket." Kamron turned the handle of the hanging basket, causing it to spin and the sticks to clack wildly as they mixed and danced inside. "I will pick a prize, then draw a winning stick. When I read out the number, if you have the matching number, hold your stick in the air, and make your way to the stage. If the number called isn't found in three minutes' time, we will redraw. All right?"

The crowd cheered and agreed. He spun the basket handle again, causing the happy clacking to sound over the crowd. He thought he heard something else under the noise but dismissed it. The basket came to a halt, and he opened the small door.

"The first prize is for the golden hairpins," Kamron announced. He reached into the basket and glanced at his father, who frowned as he looked behind the stage toward the castle.

A cry rose again, and this time the crowd murmured.

The king held up a hand and everyone went silent, tensing as if knowing something was amiss.

"Fire!"

The voice was faint but undeniable.

A sweat streaked man ran toward the crowd, his face ashen with terror. "Fire! The castle is on fire!"

# Chapter Four

"You there," the queen pointed to a woman in mage robes in the front row. "Gather the fire hose and summon the other mages."

"The what?" the woman asked.

The king moved. One moment he leaned toward the castle, straining with the rest of them to hear the call, and the next he sprinted away from Kamron, straight for the castle. Something like fear broke out across Kamron's back. He ran after his dad, desperate to make sure he didn't do something stupid, like enter the castle.

The king was old, he limped a little in winter when he didn't think anyone was looking. How the king outran him, Kamron would never know. He lost sight of the towering monarch almost immediately and raced to the back of the castle. The smoke wasn't obvious until he rounded the corner behind the stables. Flames roared as they engulfed the wooden wing. Kamron blinked twice, frozen in awe, then ran for the stables. He opened stalls and coaxed horses to run anywhere but toward the castle. The stable hands assisted him until every beast was free. They would have a miserable time collecting them from the city streets, but it would be worth it if the fire jumped to the wooden stables.

With the task done, Kamron returned to the horde of confused and panicked onlookers to find his mother at the front directing a group of mages to the main water spigot used by the castle. Lukas followed her, dragging an enormous coil of hose with the help of two other men.

"I don't understand how your predecessor didn't teach you the spells," the queen said to a harassed-looking head sorcerer.

Sorcerer Agness grimaced. "I don't think he was thinking about such things when his heart gave out, Your Majesty."

The queen sighed. "I don't have the skill to get it running, but I can explain it to you. Kamron, spread the word we need everyone with a bit of magic to come lend their strength to the spell."

Kamron nodded and set off, giving Lukas a nod while his friend attempted to attach the large hose to the spigot. He returned with a handful of mages to find the hose set up and blasting more water than seemed possible toward the fire. He found a space between his mother and Lukas to grip the hose and lend his magical strength. Kamron had never been academically trained to use his magic. His skills were better for unraveling spells than building them, but he had a good bit of strength to lend.

Lukas kept his hand on the hose, funneling his small magical gift into the spells the sorcerer ran. His face was pale and filled with fear as the orange flames reflected in his eyes. Kamron's own chest grew tight every moment the fire raged. Kamron and Lukas's magical strength ran out faster than the more powerful mages, and they stepped to the side, letting others with strength left to step in and lend their power to the spells.

Eventually, a tall figure emerged from the smoke and relief overwhelmed Kamron as his father approached his mother.

King Silas coughed, his fine tunic smeared with soot. "The castle is empty, as far as we can tell."

"The kitchens?" Kamron asked.

His father nodded. “Empty.”

Kamron relaxed slightly.

“How is it spreading so fast?” the king asked.

Queen Elodie shook her head and a nervous-looking enchanter stepped forward. “The fire proofing spells seem to have collapsed under the force of the fire.”

“How can that be?” the king asked.

The head sorcerer, slumping a little under the burden of the spell, turned her head. “Who was in charge of renewing the fire proofing spells?”

“Enchanter Cam,” a woman said.

“He retired last spring,” a third voice put in.

“Who replaced his duties?”

The mass of mages was silent for a long moment, broken only by the king’s cough. The queen looked up at him sharply. “I’m going to brew a smoke relief tonic.”

The king blocked her. “Your workroom is too close to the smoke.”

The queen glared up at her husband. “My workroom isn’t the only place in the city stocked with herbs. We will need gallons of tonic before the night is up.” The queen brushed past the mages and turned toward the city.

She wasn’t wrong. The fire burned itself out, not because of any feat of the mages, but because it eventually ran out of wood to fuel it.

In the darkness of the night, the remaining charred structure smoldered and glowed while the mages with remaining power continued to douse the embers. Kamron and Lukas helped distribute tonic to those affected by the smoke, and were part of the force finding rooms in the city for the displaced. The castle was off-limits for the night as the smoke settled, leaving the snootier courtiers and dignitaries enraged. They insisted on fresh clothes and their own belongings, but the king refused to send in any servants, saying the nobles could risk their own lives if they wished. They relented and were escorted to inns in the city or spare rooms in other nobles' townhouses.

Kamron kept working until his father ordered him to bed in a room of the Marigold tavern. The room was small with two pallet beds on either wall. Kamron sank into one, and Lukas the other. Lukas let out a deep sigh.

"I know," Kamron said, feeling every inch of the anxiety, stress, and fear his friend's breath carried. "But no one was hurt."

Lukas didn't reply, and they each sat staring at the wall for a long time.

"Let's get some sleep."

Lukas tapped off the light globe, and they each removed their boots and crawled into bed.

Over the night, the burned wooden wing attached to the castle fell into the sinkhole it had loomed over for centuries. The next morning, the queen stood on the edge of the hole, stony-faced as she stared down into the still smoking pit. Kamron approached and stood silently at her side, looking over the mess.

The remaining stone castle looked as if it had been cleaved in two and scarred with soot. The hallways filled with rugs and tapestries, now exposed to open air, were black and ruined. The destruction was expected, but it still shocked Kamron seeing his home so damaged. Kamron set to work on cleanup. Most of the remaining castle was unscathed beyond soot and smoke damage. Lukas and Kamron helped on the team boarding up the espoused hallway until they were served a lunch of simple rations.

Kamron received a summons from his parents.

On his way, he passed the head sorcerer in the hallway, and the woman didn't meet his eyes. A small sinking feeling took over his stomach, but he brushed it off as he entered his parents' sitting room without knocking. He paused when he saw his parents, unable to read their expressions. There was sadness, but more than that was closed off. Kamron could always read their expressions, and the lack now made him uneasy.

"Mum, Dad, what can I help with?"

They turned as one and looked at him, then his father looked away.

"Sorcerer Flemming has been up all night studying the ruins. He believes the fire protection spells did not deteriorate over time, but were unraveled."

"That's . . . concerning," Kamron said.

His father's jaw tightened. He was mad. Very mad.

"He believes the fire was set maliciously. Intentionally. An accelerant was used, dumped down the lining of the stone supports from the tower, allowing the fire to spread vertically first, catching and consuming as much of the structure as possible," his father said without looking at him.

His mother met his gaze. Her face was bleak, and she held out her hands. "Come here, my son."

Kamron went to her and knelt in front of her, placing his hands in hers. She squeezed his hands and met his eyes with an intensity that scared him. "I worry about you, my son, more than I've ever worried about anything in my entire life. You're smart, smarter than most around you. You can see twenty solutions to a problem where others can't find one and you possess the will needed to accomplish anything you desire." A single tear ran down the queen's cheek. "But I worry about what kind of man you will be. What kind of man can you become when you clearly care so little for any life but your own?"

Kamron blinked. "I do care."

"And I don't believe you," the queen replied. "How could you do something as dangerous and reckless as this, as if the world is a game? Do you understand how many could have died if things had gone differently yesterday?"

"Yes. I do. But no one *was* hurt, Mother." Kamron ran a hand over his hair. He knew they would be mad, but disappointed? Worried? Didn't they see what he had done? "Every person in the castle cleared out for the raffle. The entire castle was empty."

The queen's eyes widened and then narrowed again in anger. Another hot tear ran down her cheek. "Which is, of course, why you suggested everyone in the castle should enter the raffle regardless of station?"

"I care about people," Kamron insisted. "That's why I'm training to be a knight, so I can better protect them."

"I see now where we went wrong," the king said, still not meeting Kamron's eyes. "We never should have let you get away with your schemes as a child. It's taught you to be fearless and selfish. I must hope that it is not too late for you to become a better man."

Before Kamron could reply, there was a knock on the door and his aunt let herself in. Kamron stood and bowed to Dess.

"You called for me, Your Majesties?"

"Yes," the king turned to the knight, his face all stony anger. "We will move all operations to Tate for the foreseeable future." A small gong of success rung in the back of Kamron's mind, but it felt hollow. "The castle has been warned of our arrival and is making the necessary preparations. I need someone to tie up loose ends here."

Dess nodded. "I will assign Celes to the work."

Celes, Dess's oldest child, was just as commanding a leader as Dess herself, yet maybe a touch more organized and happier to work with people.

"Thank you. I also fear that your squire has begun to lack in his clerical duties," the king said. "I wish to see his abilities at work. He is to record all victims of the fire and their losses, tallying both *sentimental* and market value for the lost property and bringing each victim resolution and satisfaction to their loss."

Kamron twisted his head to his father.

"It will be done, sir," Dess said. Kamron glanced at his knight master who met his eyes evenly. "You have your orders. You are dismissed."

Kamron shot one last look back at his parents. Both masking

sadness with anger or resignation. Kamron shook his head, confused by their responses. Didn't they understand he hadn't been reckless? He'd planned. He'd been careful, and his work would benefit the kingdom in the long term. His parents just couldn't see past the damage because some people lost things. Things were replaceable, but he'd protected the people. Why didn't they see that?

With the help of his friend and fellow squire Branson, Kamron set up a table near the kitchens for people to check in with him and list what they lost. He grumbled, frustrated at his lot, while a few servants spread the word to come to him with their losses. Branson dumped a stack of blank paper on his desk, and Kamron eyed it, positive it was way more than necessary.

"I don't see what the big deal is. It's just things people have lost, it's not like any lives were lost," Kamron said. Branson paused in straightening the paper and shot an incredulous glance at Kamron, before looking away. "You disagree?" Kamron asked him.

"No," Branson replied, but there was a hardness to his mouth.

"Yes, you do."

"You'll need more ink. Let me fetch it."

"Branson, wait."

The squire paused and turned back to Kamron. "How may I serve, Prince?"

Kamron frowned. "Why are you angry? You never call me Prince."

"I've also never felt the difference in our stations as much as I do now."

"What do you mean?"

Branson shook his head and turned away. Kamron let him go, confused at his friend's reaction. They'd been friendly since they were pages, once Kamron made it clear to everyone in his class that he didn't see a difference between their roles just because he would be the king one day.

Branson made it ten paces before turning back. He stomped to

Kamron's table, red-faced, and stood tall. "You don't know what it is to go without something you need. Not having clothes that fit, not having warm blankets in the winter, and then someone gives you a quilt they made, and it's your most prized possession. When you don't have a lot, everything matters." He bit his lip and shook his fist in the air for a moment. "You'll see what I mean soon."

Branson tapped the table once and walked away, leaving Kamron frowning in his chair. He'd forgotten Branson came from a common-born background. Anyone could apply for page training, but only the best common-born were accepted. When they graduated to squires, a noble like Kamron was taken into service by a knight. His room and board paid for, but he earned no wage. Instead, he was taught and trained while serving the knight however they needed until he reached adulthood and was knighted himself. For someone like Branson becoming a squire was a full-time job. He made a living serving his knight and would never reach a higher position. But they had started as pages the same year, and had been selected as squires at the same time, so Kamron had forgotten Branson ever lived a different life.

Before long, people lined up in front of his table. They sat in the seat across from Kamron as he took their name, position, and who they worked for, if not for Aluna. Then, soot streaked and downcast, they told him all they had lost. Sometimes the lists were long and detailed, yet it was almost more disheartening when they were short.

The number of people who lost property in the fire was extensive. With the castle heavily populated with out-of-town visitors for the holiday, Kamron feared his job would never end.

His father had stressed reimbursing a sentimental value. At first, Kamron had dismissed it as frivolous, but after Branson's words, he asked each person how important the items were to them. Clothes and necessities were important, but Kamron was shocked at how frequently people described a belonging as irreplaceable. Drawings or paintings of family, trinkets from loved ones, keepsakes, love letters, and so much more.

Kamron didn't have items like these. He had items he cared about or preferred over others, but everything was replaceable. It was hard to understand the sentimental attachment these people had to everyday objects. One woman had cried over a lost cloak her grandmother had made her before passing away. Kamron didn't know her grandmother but suspected she hadn't been some revered seamstress. A new, better-quality cloak should have done just as well, but somehow it didn't.

Kamron's back ached and his fingers cramped, yet still his line stretched longer. When it got dark, some people left, but not all. He created a glowing ball of mage light and set it to hang over the table so he could still write. He thought this task would be more efficient with a host of scribes, not one lone squire with bad handwriting, but his father had a point he was trying to make, assigning the task to Kamron, and he refused to give up, or work his way out of the job until he knew what the point was. His father couldn't believe making lists would somehow make him a better man.

Eventually a tall, beautiful woman with chestnut hair and dazzling eyes, about twice Kamron's age, came out and approached his line. "Sorry everyone, it's getting late. We need to pick this back up tomorrow." A few people groaned. "I know your time is important. Squire Kamron will be back here an hour after dawn to continue taking down your losses." Kamron glared at Lady Celes, but she only smiled at him and thanked all the victims for their time.

Kamron stood and stretched, popping his back in a dozen places before collecting his papers. The stack of paper was almost full, and he would need to find a better way to carry the load.

When they were at last alone, Celes approached his table. "How did it go?"

Kamron yawned. "Mind-numbingly dull. And I have absolutely no idea how to calculate value based on sentimentality."

Celes nodded. "And remember, you can't just give everyone a lump sum. I doubt the crown coffers can handle that. You will need to replace items with items in some cases and work up payment plans with the businesses you contract with."

Kamron set down his papers and blinked up at her.

Celes grinned and patted him on the head, something she'd done since he was young. "I recommend making friends with Bernie in the castle stores. He's been supplying the castle with everything we need for the last few decades. He has a wealth of knowledge."

Kamron let out a deep breath and made a mental note to track down the older man whenever he got some free time. His stomach grumbled. How late did the Marigold's kitchens stay open? "Do you know where your mum is?"

Celes grimaced. "She got a letter that bandits struck Callin and set off north with a troop of men to help."

Kamron frowned. Bandits meant ununiformed soldiers from Vasniydor, a subtle, yet unofficial, attack as a precursor for war. Callin was a small village further south than had been hit before. He gathered up his supplies and they started back toward town. "I need to leave in the morning to meet her. I can't stay here if they are attacking."

"No, I'm under strict instructions to keep you here, and to keep you too busy to get into any trouble," Celes told him. "What on eres did you do this time to set her off? And the timing of the castle catching fire is terrible. Everyone is under enough stress as it is without you adding to it with your schemes."

Kamron didn't think she expected a reply. She knew him well; of the fifteen years she had on him, she'd spent most watching his mischief.

A sharp pain stabbed Kamron's chest and he flinched, but after a moment, it was gone. His hands shook and he fumbled his papers. What was wrong with him? He needed to get a grip on whatever emotion raced around the back of his head. It wasn't productive, so he would ignore it. He just needed sleep.

Back at the Marigold, Kamron talked a kitchen worker out of a few rolls and trudged up the stairs to his room. He stood in the doorway of the small room, and blinked at a squire he didn't know well, sitting on Lukas's bed. Kamron glanced at the number on the door, but it was the right room. He kicked closed the door and dumped everything on his bed. "Where's Lukas?"

The other squire looked nervous at Kamron's arrival. "Uh, is that the squire from Arnav who was staying here?" Kamron gave him a look, which seemed to send the right message, since the squire continued without Kamron having to say anything. "Right, well, his knight master was part of the procession that left with the king and queen this afternoon."

Kamron blinked at the man. "The king and queen left?"

"Yes, after lunch. They left with a whole host of courtiers for Tate. They packed lightly, so there's another caravan getting ready to leave by the end of the week."

Kamron sighed and set to organizing his supplies and clearing off his bed for sleep.

When he was done, he had an extra folded paper he didn't remember. Closer examination showed it was a letter from Lukas. He unraveled the small sealing charm Lukas enjoyed using because it didn't have a key and knew it was a pain to open. His eyes ran over the scribbled letter.

*Kam,*

*I'm setting out for Tate with your parents, apparently you aren't coming?! Write me when you can. Do they know? It feels like they know, but no one is saying anything. They wouldn't let me say good-bye. At least this means we were successful, right? Next time you're at the new capital, you will only be a half day's ride from me.*

*I don't feel great about what happened, and I think we need to cool it with the schemes for a while, before someone gets hurt.*

*Stay safe when you go north again.*

*-Lu*

Kamron crumpled the letter in his fist and closed his eyes. His parents had known they were leaving, and they didn't tell him, didn't even say a proper goodbye. Usually their partings included hugs and forehead kisses, which Kamron found incredibly stupid, but missed more than he could imagine. That sharp pang entered his chest again, and he pushed away the feeling. Sleep. Sleep would fix everything.

# Chapter Five

Up on the edge of a hill, overlooking the peaceful countryside, with Tross a distant figure on the horizon, Kamron lay back in the grass and studied the castle. His parents had brought him to this small clearing overlooking the city many times as a child, for picnics, or afternoon getaways when work became too much for them. Kamron sat in this exact spot, more times than he could remember, studying the castle and trying to figure out where his room was or talking about the best way to attack and defend the city with his father. He knew the castle like he knew his favorite horse. He could spot her from a distance, knew how she ran and walked, and how far she could be pushed before exhaustion.

Kamron had pushed the castle too far. He couldn't even recognize it anymore.

He wanted to write a letter to his parents, talk about how the view had changed, but would they reply? His parents used to send daily letters whenever they were apart from their son, but after the fire, since they left for Tate, he received nothing. The upper-class citizens of Tross left in the first two days after the castle fire, off to country estates or homes in other cities, with their households packing and following days after. The businesses that catered to that class of people, seeing the writing on the wall, began putting their affairs in order and packing wagons before quietly leaving the city themselves.

It took four days for Kamron to list all the losses from the castle fire. It would have only taken three, but on the third day the tallying of lost possessions became too much for him and he took a half day, lending his strength to the crew walling up the castle. A maid had cried at his table over the loss of her pet bird. She sobbed, believing her pet fell victim to the flames. Kamron knew the bird was safe, likely somewhere in the countryside enjoying his best birdy life after he'd set it free out the window during his and Lukas's check of the servants' rooms, but he couldn't tell this woman that. Instead, he sat and watched her deep grief, and the sharp pain in his chest returned with force.

Hard physical labor helped him to center himself, and he'd slept well that night.

Once the list was complete, he took it to Bernie and begged the man's help with filling the requests. That was when he found out about the merchants leaving the city. Not all had left, but the best, richest, and most prolific.

"Keep it to yourself," Bernie told him, leveling a squinted glare at Kamron. "Once word gets out, the city will unravel faster than a seagull shites in the streets."

Kamron frowned. "So, where am I supposed to get these supplies?"

"Go to the makers, of course," Bernie told him, before listing two dozen businesses, cobblers, tanners, tailors, and many more. "If you flood them with requests, perhaps you'll distract them long enough that they won't pull out of the city after the merchants."

It worked, for another week, and then the higher class of businesses unloaded everything they had on hand, took the crown's promise of repayment and future work, and left the city in droves.

Kamron didn't get how Celes kept an even temper in the wake

of the mass exodus as the middling businesses slowly followed the higher ones. Within a few months, Tross would be a graveyard with only those too poor to leave left to manage things.

Kamron sighed and flopped onto the grass. He didn't recognize the castle any longer, and not just because the wooden wing was gone.

He had to do it. Aluna suffered with the capital being so far from its allies, and with the shoddy infrastructure of the city, half the council had to be bribed to come to the city for annual meetings. It made sense for the capital to be moved, and not just so he would be close to his best friend, even if that was why he first came up with the idea. It was logical and well-planned, but Kamron now doubted his methods. He could have found a way to convince his parents to move the capital that didn't involve destroying lives and the castle. He should have waited till he was a knight and had a position of influence at court or waited till he himself was king and didn't need to convince anyone of his plans.

Instead, he'd been hasty and too convinced of his own brilliance to second guess his plan. He hadn't thought far enough ahead to ask himself what would happen to the city when the capital suddenly moved. He was lucky no one had been killed; he understood that now. If only his luck were enough to cover all his mistakes.

Once he'd wallowed long enough in his own sorrows, Kamron pulled his horse, Lightning, away from her lunch of summer clover, and rode back to the city. A messenger found him in the stables with a note that Celes was looking for him. He left Lightning in the hands of a stable girl and found Celes in her sitting room, listening to a report from a clerk. She waved him in when he knocked.

"Without the merchants, the city will perish," the clerk said, and Kamron's stomach did a little dance. "We cannot move supplies or stores without them. The infrastructure of the capital was built on trade and commerce."

"But without the trade of the fall harvest, most of the merchants will lose money. They can't possibly think they can make up the commission in other cities," Celes said.

The clerk shrugged. "Either they have plans, or they didn't think that far ahead. Everyone is panicking at the change in situation."

"You don't have to tell me that," Celes said under her breath. "Can we expect the merchants back when the harvest is coming in?"

The clerk shook his head. "Some of them have set out on their seasonal routes early, heading into the upper Twoshy, and it will be months before they return. All of them have completely cleared out their warehouses in the city before departing."

Celes frowned. "Why would they clear out completely? Do they never expect to return?"

The clerk's jaw tightened, and he stood a little straighter. Kamron braced himself. This wouldn't be good news. "My sources indicate Synclare was the first, and the rest followed his actions. He may have shared a prediction with the others that caused the panic."

Celes stilled for a beat before letting out a slow, controlled breath. "What did he say?"

"He predicted there would be rioting before the summer ends and that more than just the castle would be in flames long before the leaves fall."

Celes closed her eyes. "Thank you, Semus."

"There's one more thing, my lady," the clerk added, looking grim.

"Let's hear it."

"Some of the more prolific members of Tross's underworld are also reported to have left."

Celes rolled her eyes. "And the rats only flee before a disaster. Right. Thanks again, Semus."

The clerk turned on his heels and left. Celes, not looking at

Kamron, flopped back into a chair and stared up at the ceiling. "Any ideas?"

"Any what?" Kamron asked, not sure she spoke to him.

Celes snorted and turned her head to Kamron. "You're the brilliant one in the room, aren't you? Any idea how to save the city?"

Kamron thought for a long moment. He stared out the window and chewed on his cheek. The window looked out onto the west fields, where farms stretched into the distance for acres and acres. As the biggest country in the Twoshy, Tross accounted for more than thirty percent of the continent's food production. If the harvest couldn't be moved and sold, Aluna's economy would crash, and every country in the Twoshy would feel the food shortages. "The farmers and workers haven't left. Have those who process the harvest?"

"No, only those who buy, sell, trade, and most importantly, transport the harvest."

Kamron nodded. "But not all the merchants have left, right?"

"No, I'm sure some of the shadier sorts are still here, and the paupers."

Kamron shot her a look. "My mother and yours would skin you alive if they heard you say that."

"Yes, but they aren't here, and you know I'm right. They aren't worth much in comparison."

Kamron frowned. Was she right? Kamron's mom had told him many stories of her time as a child, playing with those who lived in the lower city. She said most of the people who their class looked down upon and called criminals were ten times harder working than anyone else. They were the lifeblood of any city. Kamron knew his auntie Callie had started her life on the streets and Healer Beathan, who his mom took spiced turnovers to every winter solstice, had dedicated her life to helping those in the lower city. She would never leave, even if everyone with two coins to rub together did.

Kamron took a deep breath and turned back to Celes. "We use the merchants who stayed."

Celes shook her head. "They can't support the volume of goods we produce each year. It's not realistic. Synclare has twenty-nine wagons in his business alone."

"Send word to the new capital to send back our wagons once they've arrived and unloaded. Tate has plenty of wagons and carriages already. Adding everything we've just brought over, their city will be overflowing. We can lend out our wagons to the merchants remaining and write up contracts, so it's just for the season while they work for us. If they manage things well, they can buy themselves new wagons or buy ours when the season is over. They will build thriving businesses, and we will earn their loyalty, so they stay with the city once the smoke has cleared."

Celes raised her eyebrows. "And you trust the remaining merchants to handle the work honorably as well as competently?"

"Don't you have a sister-in-law or cousin who's the head of a merchant family in Qosha? Ask her to lend us someone who works well with the lower class and can offer advice to our merchants as they scale up their businesses. That way, it won't feel like we're controlling their every move." Kamron sat in a velvet chair as he thought through the details. "We can ask people we trust that have a good pulse on the city who they recommend we work with. Callie of the Marigold and the head healer of the Odure clinic are my recommendations."

Celes let out a deep breath. "It could work."

Kamron nodded. "There are always people looking for work in the Odure district. This will provide jobs on top of everything else, helping to boost the economy. We need to show the city the castle isn't dying, just changing."

"My family will be here within two weeks." Celes met Kamron's eyes. "Your parents have assigned me the steward of the castle for the foreseeable future."

Kamron nodded. With the capital moving, someone had to

look over Tross and manage all the business the castle oversaw. It was a huge honor and a huge pile of work. Kamron didn't envy Celes in the slightest. Then an idea popped into his head. He grinned. "You should hit up some of the remaining tailors and request new wardrobes for the girls."

Celes frowned. She had three young daughters who liked mischief almost as much as Kamron did. "To give them business?" Celes asked.

"No, to send a message. The styles are just different enough between here and Lacanto they will stand out as is. By getting them, and yourself, a new wardrobe in the style of Tross, you send the message that you both want to be here and plan to stay."

Celes stood, a small spark in her eyes that had been missing the last few days. "This might work." She turned to Kamron. "Keep the ideas coming."

"I will."

She nodded, and her smile grew a little apprehensive. "I also wanted to tell you I had a letter from my mom."

Kamron's heart beat a little faster. Was he getting out? Back to his proper life as a squire? "Did Dess have any orders for me?" The silence from his knight master was nearly as suffocating as the silence from his own parents.

"Yes, but not the sort you are looking for. There's a builder just arrived from Pundica who will be working on the castle. She's loaned him your service for as long as he needs it. He's a bit older, so I expect it will be a lot of lifting and fetching." She grimaced. "Sorry, I know it's not what you were hoping."

Kamron shook his head. "It's fine. I will help however I can."

Celes nodded, and Kamron took it as his cue to leave. He took the long way out of the castle and wandered around to the construction site on the east. The new builder would likely be unpacking or resting after his journey, but perhaps his people would be setting up at the worksite. The work on boarding up the exposed halls of the castle had been completed for some time, and they'd set up a small rail around the sinkhole to keep people from falling in. He wondered what else the builder was needed for.

Two large wagons sat in the construction site, and several people unloaded supplies closer to the castle.

An older, lean, black man, maybe in his sixties or so, carried a big sack on each shoulder, as if they were filled with feathers. Kamron recognized him immediately.

"Good, you're here. Take these to the edge of the sinkhole."

"Uncle Thomas! What are you doing here?" Kamron asked, surprised to see one of his mom's oldest friends.

Instead of replying, Thomas transferred the large sacks to Kamron's shoulders. He sagged under the weight but carried his burdens to a small pile growing on the edge of the sinkhole. A tall woman with pale skin and red hair climbed over the guardrail as Kamron approached. She held a rope tied off on one of the castle's supports, and as Kamron watched, she grinned at him and hopped down into the sinkhole.

A familiar-looking man leaned against the guardrail, watching with a bored expression.

"Come along, there's more in the wagon," Thomas said behind Kamron as he unloaded more sacks, as if they weighed nothing. Kamron jogged a little to catch up to Thomas's long stride, refusing to be outdone by the older man. Kamron was drenched in sweat by the time they finished unloading, and the workers gathered at the sinkhole. There were six newcomers, including Thomas. The bored man watching for the redhead was Thomas's nephew, Van, who Kamron hadn't seen since he was little. He grinned and pulled Kamron into a hug when he realized who he was. The redhead in the hole was his wife, Lavender. Then there was Sara, a short woman who'd somehow carried four sacks at once, Alex and Cisco, a brother and sister who looked similar with their golden-brown complexion and straight black hair. And the last in their group was Bran, a gruff-looking man whose two fingers on his left hand were missing. After the introductions, no one said anything until

Lavender climbed the rope out of the sinkhole, and Van gave her a hand onto steady ground.

"It's Dwarv work, for sure," Lavender said, gesturing to the sinkhole. Kamron frowned. He knew Tross was originally home to Dwarvman, one of the races of people who occupied their world, but they were known for their excellent stonework. If they made tunnels, they wouldn't collapse.

Thomas nodded. "That's what I suspected when I helped stabilize this wing a few decades ago. Is everything inactive now?"

"Yes. The tunnels were rigged to collapse, for sure, but everything that was booby-trapped to collapse has done so."

Kamron shook his head. "Wait, do you mean the sinkhole was planned by the Dwarv?"

"Yes," Lavender said. "They would have been put in place centuries ago. You still get new ones from time to time, right?" Kamron nodded and Lavender looked at Thomas. "We'll need to do more investigating around the city, but the ground here is solid. We'll need to excavate some of the burned mess down here. There's some of the original stone we can use to rebuild if we can set up a pulley to get it out, but I think adding about seven or eight supports down in the tunnels will stabilize it and we can close up this hole."

Thomas nodded. "The kid will help in the pit. Teach him how we run the supports."

"Kid." The term made Kamron smile. Kids was what they called baby goats, but Thomas, like Kamron's mom, also used it to refer to young people. Thomas, like Kamron's mom, had grown up in another world. They, and a few dozen others, were known as the Misplaced Children, though they were all old-timers now, many with grandchildren. Kamron grew up hearing stories of their life on Earth, another world, or an imaginary illusion dreamed up by an evil wizard, depending on who you asked. When they were young, most of the Misplaced traveled back and forth between Earth and their birth world, Eres, as the spell trapping them on

Earth began to break down. Eventually, a group of them, including Thomas and his mom, got together and broke the spell that kept them captive, and now they were free to live on Eres in peace.

The evil wizard who trapped them still lived in the Tokke Mountains to the south of Aluna, and he was the source of another set of stories his mother told him. He had wronged his mother greatly, and yet Queen Elodie told Kamron of a vow she made to the old, evil wizard. *I vow to leave these mountains, and that neither I nor anyone in my line will bother you again unless you come to us first.* It was an old story. One he didn't think of often, yet he found the words still sat perfectly intact in his memory.

The smile at Thomas's word choice vanished as Kamron realized what Thomas had actually said. "Wait, you mean I need to go down in the pit?"

"Will that be a problem?" Thomas asked.

Kamron shook his head, and Thomas turned back to the group to finish laying out plans. When the others left to start on their projects, Thomas turned to Kamron, his expression hard and disapproving. "Do you know why you'll be working under me for the time being?"

Kamron grimaced. "Yes, do you?"

"Yes. Your mom spoke to me directly." Thomas crossed his arms. "Are you going to give me any trouble?"

Kamron sighed and leaned against the railing. "No. I see now what I did was stupid and reckless. I just want to do whatever I can to fix things and keep Tross from tearing itself apart."

"Good." He clasped Kamron on the shoulder. "I told your mom it was the mistake of a shortsighted teenager, and not one of someone lacking empathy for all sentient beings. I'm glad I wasn't wrong."

Kamron didn't disagree. He had been shortsighted, and it hurt knowing his mom feared he lacked empathy. He winced as the sharp pain hit again in his chest.

Thomas squeezed his shoulder again. "It's all right. You should feel remorse over your actions. What you did was an atrocity, and you need to feel that. But don't let it stop you. Learn from this and do better next time. You do know there were like a dozen better ways you could have done this, right?"

Kamron looked up at him. Did he have to rub salt in the wound?

Thomas sighed and leaned back on the railing next to Kamron. "I've been telling your mom for years we needed to tear down this wing so we could patch up the sinkhole properly, but it was too big of a logistical lift to empty the castle for the work, and back then your parents were putting an end to slavery in Aluna. After that, tensions with Vasniydor picked up, and the timing didn't seem right to move the capital." Thomas gave Kamron a knowing look. "It was going to happen eventually, but it didn't need to happen like this."

Kamron looked down, unable to meet the man's eyes any longer. He didn't realize how lucky he'd been. The only people who knew his crimes had left the city, leaving him to his own private remorse. Having someone who knew looking down on him made things that much harder.

He thought often about writing his parents, and while he sometimes put pen to paper, he never sent them. He had a small stack of old letters in his room from his last trip away from home before the fire. He'd seen their daily letters as trivial. Now in the silence, he reread the letters when he felt particularly down, and they became cherished objects. He couldn't imagine losing that last connection to his parents just because some privileged teenager wanted to move closer to his best friend.

Kamron could only hope one day he would do enough to pay back his wrongs.

Thomas stood. "Come, let's go talk to this new steward about job postings so we can rebuild this castle of yours."

They didn't just repair the sinkhole under the now demolished east wing of the castle. Lavender, who Kamron suspected more and more was at least part Dwarv, dismantled one hundred fourteen additional booby traps that would have continued making sinkholes through the city over the next few centuries. The Dwarv, apparently, liked to play the long game when it came to revenge.

"Will anyone be mad you fixed this?" Kamron asked her one night as they finished up work on a large sinkhole in the Prole District.

Lavender shrugged. "Whoever came up with the trick has long since had their revenge on your ancestors. Now it only hurts innocent people."

Kamron nodded. He wasn't proud of his family's history. It had been his ancestor who convinced the others to colonize the Twoshy, but Wulfram hadn't risen from the battle unscathed as one of the last great Elvman kings marked him and his line with a curse. Kamron rubbed the albatross birthmark on his forearm and got back to work.

Repairing the city's sinkholes was a massive undertaking. It required stone, cement, wood for framing, tools, and an endless list of supplies, most of which Tross didn't have on hand in the quantities needed. It put the city's newest head merchants to the test as Celes enacted Kamron's plan and wrote up contracts with the merchants who usually catered to a much smaller clientele.

Kamron met with Celes several times a week, sometimes with others like Callie's oldest son, Mav, who had taken on many of her businesses or with someone Healer Beathan sent along to inform them of the pulse of the city. There were more fights than usual for the summer as tensions ran high and the city emptied, but meticulously they replaced key industries, either by bringing in someone trusted or by lifting up smaller businesses in the city.

Fixing the sinkhole at the castle was a more complex task, as so many decades of debris had fallen in and needed to be moved or removed.

Thomas's vision for the castle required them to excavate the original stone that had been part of the castle when the sinkhole first opened. He wasn't adding any new structure, instead he wanted to replace the boarded-up walls with true stone and mortar so that the castle would remain as it was, but would be secure and truly protected from the elements.

Work slowed as available workers switched to the higher priority job of bringing in the harvest, and the city held their breath to see if the new, smaller, and less important Tross could handle its own.

In the midst of the harvest, Kamron ventured out to the surrounding farms and lent a hand. As a boy, his mother took him to help in the harvest so he would better understand the work it took for their country to prosper. He knew the basic tasks, but he wasn't very good at most of them. He was terrible with a sickle, never managing the right angle, but he could thresh grains like the best of them. And there was always a need to carry heavy things, which Kamron excelled at.

When at the farms, he checked in on the workers. With less oversight than previous years, there was a rise in reports of worker mistreatment. Kamron thrashed wheat and listened to the field gossip about where working conditions might not be hospitable, and suggested members of the Alunan guard in charge of investigating farm owners check in on things. It wasn't much, and they couldn't catch everything, but it made a difference for the people trying to make a living on the seasonal work.

And Kamron sort of loved the gossip. He knew plenty of interest about many of the elite around Aluna, and he was always properly shocked to learn how much servants or the relatives of servants knew in exchange.

"And that's why the Lord and Lady of Capnor sleep on different floors," Masy, an older woman with wiry gray hair, said as she lifted a full basket of wheat grains onto her hip. "But you didn't hear it from me." She waggled a finger as she strutted away from their threshing stone.

Kamron snorted and got back to work. He couldn't wait to

write to his parents and see if they knew about what went on in Capnor. A small pang jabbed in Kamron's chest. He'd forgotten again. He wouldn't be writing his parents anything when they had so clearly cut communication with him. He would write Lukas instead. His best friend would still find it interesting, even if he didn't know the people involved.

"Oi, lad. Pick up the pace. I wanna eat lunch on time today."

Kamron blinked and looked up at the man collecting another full basket of wheat. Kamron resumed threshing, not realizing he'd slowed.

"What bird stole your bread?" Lea, another older woman Kamron liked to learn new curse words from, asked.

"It's nothing," Kamron said, forcing a smile onto his face. Lea didn't look convinced. "So, what plans do you have once the harvest is over?"

"You mean if we manage to get everything in on time, and those green merchants manage to sell everything, and our overlords pay us what we've been promised?" Lea asked with a skeptical look at Kamron. Richie, Dann, and Laural, all working around Kamron, snorted or laughed. Lea loved to prod Kamron's positive outlook on the state of the economy. Everyone knew things were teetering on the edge, but Kamron believed they would be successful.

"Yes, exactly," Kamron said.

Lea snorted. "I plan to buy enough food to get me through winter, get my roof fixed, and save anything left over for when I'm forced to leave Tross."

"Come now, Lea. It won't come to that. The lad here will make sure of it." He gestured to Kamron. "Isn't that right?" Richie said, flashing a grin with a few missing teeth.

"Now that sounds like a boring way to celebrate your hard work," Dan said to Lea. "Aren't you gonna celebrate even a little when the harvest is over? Go out for a drink, bake a pie, buy a nice cut of roast?"

As the breeze died down, the chaff on their threshing stone began to build up, and Kamron picked up an empty basket to fan away some of the mess.

"Why would I waste my hard earnings on something that might taste good for five minutes when I could use it to keep my head dry through winter?" Lea asked.

Masy returned in time to hear the end of the conversation and shook her head as she set down a stack of empty baskets. "Some of us need a little joy to get us through the hard times, you old loon," she said to Lea. "How about you, Laural?" she asked the younger girl who didn't tend to voice her opinion without invitation. "What will you buy when you have a little extra?"

Laural ducked her head. "I've been running low on paints. I need more yellow."

"Now that sounds like a proper celebration," Masy said, nodding to the girl.

"What do you like to paint?" Kamron asked. He thought she might clam up, as she usually did when he addressed her, but was relieved to see a far-off look of joy enter her eyes.

"Landscapes, mostly. Or cityscapes. Tross has changed so much the last few months that I've been comparing it to my old work, and can hardly believe it sometimes."

Kamron nodded. He knew what she meant. It was more than just the castle. As the upper districts emptied of the wealthier citizens and businesses, the lower ring of the city had flourished in small, surprising ways. The only cobbler left in the city was able to hire a carpenter to patch up his roof and expand to the collapsing building next door, which he rebuilt better than new. The carpenter, now in higher demand took on six new apprentices who all were hired out to rebuild flourishing businesses. The Odure district was recognizable by its full gutters and buildings that tended to lean one direction or the other, but without the waste from the upper rings, the gutters could manage just fine, and more and more buildings had fresh paint and straight walls.

"If you paint a good view of the castle once the work on the east end is complete, let me know. I'd love to have something accurate," Kamron told her. He could send it to his parents. They would love it.

His chest tightened and he grasped for something to focus on and clear his mind. Celebrations were important. Could he do something with that?

"What if we had our own celebration when the harvest is over?" Kamron asked. The others looked at him as if he spoke another language.

"You mean, like the six of us?" Dan asked.

Kamron laughed. "I mean all of Tross. A celebration thrown for the city to welcome winter and commend the work of everyone who helped rebuild the city and bring in the harvest."

Lea rolled her eyes and Richie made a rude comment, but Masy got an interested look in her eye. "A celebration just for those of us here now?" she asked, and Kamron knew what she meant and grinned.

"Exactly. We'll invite anyone currently in the city, and those in the fields and farms like us. Anyone in the capital can find out about it after the fact," Kamron said, and Masy cackled and had to explain it to Dan and Laural.

"He means to exclude the nobles and wealthy who deserted Tross," she told them.

Kamron grinned at Masy. "Wanna help me plan it?"

He pitched the idea to Celes a week later, who agreed. They wouldn't invite anyone outside of the city, even his parents. Instead, this would be a celebration for the city.

His sixteenth birthday passed without issue or notice in late fall. He suspected Celes knew because she sent him to work hauling stone for the castle, and he was thankful for it, as the work kept him too busy and too exhausted to lament on his own self-pity. A week later, he received a letter from Lukas, wishing him all the joys, and asking why he hadn't written lately. Lukas hinted about hoping to see him in a month, but Kamron didn't speculate on what his best friend might mean. He was done with schemes for the foreseeable future.

Kamron folded the letter and tucked it in his pocket before getting back to work. Lukas's letter was late because he thought Kamron was back in the border camps with Dess. He didn't know he was still on castle rebuilding duty. His parents knew, however. Which meant their letter wishing him a happy birthday wasn't late, it just wasn't coming. It was his first birthday ever to go unnoticed. On his first birthday as a squire away from home, his parents had even made a special trip to the border camp to surprise him. He could write to them first, send one of a dozen letters he'd written, but would it make a difference? He didn't think he could handle the rejection if they didn't reply.

The first day of winter arrived, and the celebration was perfect. They hired the best bakers in the city to make enough pastries for everyone, and the atmosphere was triumphant. Masy planned games and organized a raffle, and Laural revealed a portrait of the new castle, highlighting the change Tross had undergone. The city had worked hard, and in the end, they proved they still had a role in Aluna's economy. They would survive and prosper as they were. Other merchants would be back, but they would find less business in Tross than they might expect.

Kamron made his way through the crowd to a booth selling cider and pulled out a coin for two.

"We need to stop meeting this way."

Kamron spun about, not believing his ears. "Lady Dess." He blinked, not sure what to say.

"Yer drinks," the stall worker called, and Kamron snatched up the drinks, handing one to Dess.

"Thank you. Who's that one for?"

"Your daughter."

"Good. Will you show me where she is?"

Kamron nodded and led the way. He'd never had a hard time finding words to share with Dess, but that was back when their relationship was carefree and easy. Before she became one more person disappointed in him and abandoned him to time. The six months that passed after the fire felt like an insurmountable wall between them.

"Celes says you've done some great things for the city," Dess said, breaking the silence. "She says you staved off a riot."

Kamron shook his head. "She exaggerates, and it was a group effort." He stepped quickly through a few revelers and found Celes at a table with Thomas. He deposited her drink with a bow and turned to Dess. "Lady Knight." He bowed again and made to exit the gathering, but a strong grip on his tunic stopped him.

"Just a moment, Kam," Dess said before releasing him. "Meet me at the stables two hours after dawn. Pack for inn hopping and at least one snooty political function I'll try to avoid."

Kamron blinked. "Yes, sir."

Dess nodded once, releasing him, and he scurried off before someone else could tip his world upside down. He walked for a while in a blur, navigating through the crowd, unable to believe that he was finally free. He would finally get back on the road to their northern camp and the border scrimmage with Vasniydor, and perhaps he could do something brave to risk his life and earn back favor with his parents.

He set off toward the castle to pack. Inn hopping meant they would stop at roadside inns along the way, and wouldn't need tents or cooking gear, which was a relief since winter had set in quickly.

He debated packing the year-old letters from his parents he'd read often in the last few months. He would miss them if he kept them at the castle, but on the road they were susceptible to water damage, and he didn't want to lose his last link to his parents.

Morning came and Kamron rose earlier than needed, as he usually did, to ready both his and Dess's horses. Dess rolled into the stables right at the agreed upon time, sharing only grunts with Kamron as she mounted her horse, Dancer, and they left the castle heading north. They left the city behind without a word, and the morning burned to a crisp early winter afternoon as they reached the point where the Great Highway continued north, and a road branched east toward Tate and the rest of the country. Kamron sighed and kept his horse on the straight path.

It took him a moment to realize Dess did not.

"Where are you going?" Kamron asked, his first words of the day, as he brought Lightning to a stop.

"Where does it look like I'm going?" Dess called, not stopping as she turned east.

"But base camp is north," Kamron shouted.

"I'm not going to base camp."

Kamron shook his head and turned Lightning, nudging her into a trot till he caught up to Dess. Excitement raced over his skin, but he wasn't sure how he felt.

"This doesn't mean I forgive you," Dess said.

"The king and queen don't want to see me," Kamron said.

"What makes you think that?"

"They haven't written."

Dess turned in her saddle and gave him a flat stare. "In six months?"

Kamron couldn't help the sharp ache in his chest and the wince it forced on his face. Dess knew how many letters his parents used to send before the castle went up in flames. Mages had developed magical glass orbs that could provide immediate communication, both sight and sound from vast distances away, but orbs weren't permitted to squires. They were used more for strategic military communication or for chatting with friends or family if you had enough money or a mage friend. But for the prince of the kingdom, his parents would not break the rules. Instead, they sent letters. Frequent and numerous letters.

His mother would write him a letter one day, and his father

would feel she didn't convey his greetings well enough and would write a second letter, sending it the same day. Then after dinner his mother might have something else to add or maybe a new herb she'd developed in her garden that she wanted him to put in his tea or under his helmet for good luck, or just so he smelled nice.

It was a lot.

But it made him feel loved, and he wouldn't trade it for anything, even if the soldiers did make fun of him and his constant stack of mail.

But that was before the castle went up in flames. Six months of silence was so unheard of. He started having nightmares that his parents died while in Tate, and Kamron woke knowing he would see Celes with a black armband in mourning at lunch. But the bad news never came. Instead, it was just silence, and it was painful.

"What about your birthday?" Dess asked.

Kamron didn't reply, and Dess cursed.

"You didn't write either," Kamron reminded her.

"Yes, but I'm your knight commander. I'm supposed to put you through the ringer and heap on punishments when you've earned it."

They were silent for a long time before curiosity got the better of Kamron.

"So, where are we going?"

Dess only smiled.

# Chapter Six

Never, in the three weeks they journeyed east, did Kamron suspect his knight master would take him to a party. And not just any party. As they rolled through the gates of the most beautiful castle in the Twoshy, all elegant white stone carved to resemble living branches shaping the skyline with soft lines and arches. Kamron counted the date on his fingers over again. He still could not believe Dess had taken him to his best friend's birthday party.

The grounds before the castle of Arnav were chaotic and more crowded than Kamron had ever seen them. Carriages formed a line before the castle entryway. Men, women, and younger women Kamron's age flocked about with wide eyes while servants unloaded trunks and other parcels and luggage.

Kamron and Dess stopped in the middle of the carriages and observed the chaos for a few moments before someone spotted them and whistled for assistance. Stable hands took their mounts, while a harassed footman showed them to Dess's rooms. She had a suite as a guest of honor, and Kamron would sleep in a small room attached to hers as her lowly squire. Kamron bristled with curiosity over the amount of activity at the castle and was desperate to find out how his best friend got him here, though it seemed rude to ask Dess and deprive Lukas of the opportunity to boast.

Luckily, he didn't have long to wait. Kamron unpacked for Dess, as was his duty, laying a sparkly dress out on a magical clothes press while she enjoyed a hot bath. The party was a few hours away, and both their clothes were exquisitely wrinkled. Once her things were unpacked and in the wardrobe, Kamron tossed her saddle bags behind a desk and called it a day.

"That better not be my sword belt thunking around in there!" Dess called from her bath.

"No, your sword belt is hanging on the chair," Kamron called back.

"Nice and polished?"

Kamron sighed and got out a polishing rag—his weapon of choice as a squire.

A knock sounded through the suite, and Kamron opened the door. Two arms engulfed him in a tight hug.

"What took you so long?" Lukas asked, breaking away and flopping on a couch in the sitting room, without invitation.

"It's amazing you think we took too long when I didn't even know for sure where we were coming till we turned down the palace road."

"Dess didn't tell you?"

"Does she ever?"

They laughed, then Lukas punched Kamron in the stomach lightly, drawing a breath from his friend. "Why didn't you return any of my letters?"

Kamron sighed. "It's a long story."

"One I would rather not be a part of," Dess called from the bathroom.

Kamron and Lukas grinned at each other like idiots and moved into the hallway. Lukas lead the way to his own chambers as they dodged servants and guests. Finally Lukas ducked out of the castle into a courtyard to escape the congestion in the halls.

"So what exactly is all this about?" Kamron asked, as he reached out and splashed a fountain they passed in the small garden. The frigid water splattered down Lukas's back and his friend let out a little shriek that brought a grin to Kamron's face. "I don't remember any of your past birthdays being so crowded."

Lukas looked back at him and rolled his eyes, then he flinched at something over Kamron's shoulder.

"Ah, Prince Lukas, what a surprise running into you."

Kamron sighed, and they came to a stop while a shorter man with a large, bushy mustache approached. They had practically jogged through the halls, pretending they hadn't heard the few people who'd called out to Lukas, but here in the empty garden it would be obvious and rude.

"Lord Cern." Lukas bowed.

"You just missed my daughter. She's so excited to meet you," the lord said, before looking around as if hoping to spot her.

"What a shame. I'll make sure I stop by and say hello properly tonight. If you'll excuse me, my guest and I are—"

"Ah, Prince Kamron, is it?" Lord Cern asked before bowing. Kamron returned the bow, though he'd never met the man before.

Lukas straightened his posture, his role as host now unavoidable. "Lord Cern, may I introduce my guest, Squire Kamron of Aluna. Squire Kamron, it's my pleasure to introduce you to Lord Cern of Capis and Skuna."

Kamron bowed again, not letting his surprise cross his face. Capis, the capital of Skuna, was a massive merchant hotbed, and based on the amount of gold embroidery on this man's tunic and the several rings he wore, Kamron wouldn't be surprised to find he was very rich. But what was he doing in Rohap? "It's a pleasure to meet you," Kamron said.

"Yes, yes, of course. I'm so pleased to hear you are in attendance tonight, and I'm confident my daughter will be as well." The older man grinned and wiggled his eyebrows. Kamron nodded again.

Lukas made their excuses, and they headed for the entrance of the castle closer to Lukas's rooms.

"Is his daughter someone important?" Kamron asked, still confused by the interaction.

"I doubt it," Lukas muttered, before dodging another footman and taking the stairs to the next floor.

When at last they reached the peace of Lukas's rooms, it was Kamron's turn to flop onto a couch and stretch out by the fire. He stared up into the beautiful wooden-paneled carving of trees that extended onto the ceiling, as he'd done many times before in this exact room, on this exact chair. He took in a deep breath and let it out slowly. The room even smelled the same, and pressure built in the back of Kamron's eyes; the familiarity of it all bringing him to the verge of tears.

He'd moved back into his old rooms in Tross, only days after the fire, but the castle had never again felt like home. It just wasn't the same without his parents. But Arnav? It was exactly as Kamron had last seen it. He felt all at once like he'd been transported back to simpler times before he and Lukas dragged jugs of oil to the top of the east tower.

"Tell me," Lukas prompted. And Kamron did. His friend listened and didn't judge. Then he shared his own stress and anxiety after the fire.

"I think about what we did, and I can't believe it half the time," Lukas said, his voice soft. "I know no one got hurt, but the confidence we had . . . It was idiotic. We were lucky. Not smart."

Kamron shook his head. "Healer Beathan, my mum's old mentor, I think she knows what happened. She told me our minds don't finish developing till we're in our twenties, so youth sometimes make stupid irrational choices." Kamron ran a hand over his face. "I have a hard time accepting that. We were rational and logical, but it was wrong. I know in my chest it was the wrong move, but I can't figure out how we missed that in our planning."

"We forgot about the sanctity of life," Lukas said. "We treated it like a game when it was life and death."

Kamron was silent for a long moment. He knew Lukas was right, but he didn't want to admit he hadn't seen the people whose lives he altered as anything more than game pieces. He knew individually that everyone mattered and was important, but he'd forgotten it when looking at the big picture.

"We can't do that," Lukas continued. "Not as men who will someday be knights and then kings. If we are going to have people's lives in our hands, we have to put every life first."

They both silently agreed to be better, before one of them made a joke. Then they moved to lighter topics, like the over the top, ridiculous party Lukas had agreed to let his parents throw for him, under the condition that they invite Knight Candescence as a guest of honor.

"Why did they want to make such a big deal out of this birthday?" Kamron asked.

Lukas shook his head.

Lukas's parents were loving, much as Kamron's were, and loved to celebrate their children, but they didn't usually throw balls and invite dignitaries from all over the Twoshy for their birthdays. And what interest did the guests have in traveling so far just for a sixteen-year-old's birthday?

"They weren't very clear on that part, but I think it has something to do with my dad meeting my mom on his sixteenth birthday."

Lukas grimaced, and Kamron grinned. "Oh my. Do you think they plan to set you up with every eligible maiden? Make you fill your dance card until you find *the one*?"

Lukas threw a pillow at his face. "This isn't one of those fairy princess tales your mother used to tell us from her illusion when we were kids. Cinder-whatever." Lukas groaned. "Remember, I'm doing this for you, so you better help me dodge the crown chasers before I remind them you're just as available as I am."

Kamron froze as the realization hit him. Was he in the eligible bachelor category? He thought about the eager look Lord Cern had worn. A part of him wanted to slink back to the border camp where he didn't need to think about these things, and the only women he interacted with carried swords and scared him a little. "Maybe we should skip the party."

Lukas chuckled. "Okay, you tell my parents."

They laughed, and like that, it was as if no time had passed since the last time they were together. The afternoon disappeared too fast, and before long, Kamron went back to his room to bathe and change. The hallways were empty as the partygoers spent the remaining hour getting ready. He knocked before entering Dess's sitting room, where a maid was busy pinning up gray and blond ringlets all over Dess's head.

"Did you have fun?"

"Yes, Auntie Dess." Kamron leaned in to kiss her cheek.

"Pugh! You need to go bathe before you end up making the ballroom stink like horse," Dess said, recoiling from him.

"You know I've never really minded the smell."

"Yes, but the ladies will mind."

"So? I have two years till I'm of age, and even then I'm in no rush to marry. What does it matter now?"

Dess and the maid traded a glance that Kamron couldn't read, which he found annoying.

Dess shrugged. "It doesn't unless it does. Go get cleaned up."

Kamron gave the women an exaggerated bow, and the maid giggled. He gathered up his nice clothes and disappeared into the bathroom. He stood for a long time under the hot falling rain of the shower, one of the better evolutions of magical technology. Not a new invention. It had been around so long most small houses in the country even sported one, but Tross did not. The magical plumbing at the castle was too old, and the foundations of the city, too unstable to upgrade. Kamron wondered if Thomas's team could fix it. He would send a letter to Celes.

He hoped when this party was over he would return with Dess to the border, as he was desperate to get back to something more routine than running a city, but that didn't mean he'd abandon Tross.

He took his time getting ready, knowing as much as Dess had rushed on their trip east, she would be just as happy being late to the ball. Besides, being late meant they wouldn't have to wait in the introductory line as long.

"Now don't you look as good as new," Dess said as Kamron emerged from the bathroom, tucked into his nicest squire uniform.

"And you, my lady, are the stunner of the night," he said, bowing lavishly and offering his hand.

Dess cackled and slapped his palm. He straightened and grinned as she returned to painting her nails with a deep blue lacquer that matched her dress. "I should only be an hour or so."

Kamron rolled his eyes and flopped onto a lounge chair. "Wake me when you're ready."

He let out a deep breath and tried to force a nap, but it didn't immediately come. Formal balls could easily run into the early morning, and while he knew Dess would leave early, he wanted to have the energy to stay up with Lukas. After the last few weeks on the road, he was tired, and a quick power nap would go a long way to boosting his energy.

The sounds of light movement reached his ears before Dess picked up his hand, and a cold pressure ran over the nail on his index finger. The chemical smell of Dess's nail lacquer hit his nose.

Kamron sighed. "The color will clash with my tunic."

"Yes, but it will go so nicely with mine."

Kamron snorted but didn't protest. Dess's family colors were orange and brown, so as her squire, he wore a uniform of her house colors. A brown tunic, with an orange panel on the left side, and orange trim on his brown pants. It was supposed to unify him as her squire, though she rarely wore her own colors. As this was a dress uniform, it sported fine embroidery at the collar and hem in orange. The tunic, like all of his clothes, was designed for the sleeves to be perpetually cuffed to the elbow, revealing the birthmark on his forearm. Aluna's heirs had suffered through some unfortunate styles to show off their heritage and the curse over the generations. There was a portrait of one such relative wearing a crop top to show off the mark on his hairy belly.

Well, there had been a portrait of him once. It hung in the wooden side of the castle, so Kamron supposed it was gone now.

After applying a quick drying spell to their nails, Kamron and Dess made their way to the staging room off the great hall. Luckily, the introductory line was only three people deep.

Kamron gave their names to the announcer and held out his arm for his auntie. Dess placed her arm on his, and they stood at the open door of the great hall as the buzzing of the crowd below rose and engulfed them. The announcer took a step forward and spoke in a deep, booming voice. "Presenting Lady Knight Candescence of Lacanto in Aluna, honored guest of His and Her Majesties, escorted by her squire, Prince Kamron of Aluna."

They stepped forward as one onto the gleaming balcony, high over the wash of color that made up the guests waiting below, and slowly made their way to the grand staircase leading to the floor of the ballroom. Decorum said patient measured steps were the proper way to arrive, but Kamron found it tedious.

"You're not too embarrassed escorting an old bird to a ball, are you?" Dess asked.

Kamron snorted. "An old bird who can still beat me ten out of ten times? Please. It is and will always be an honor." Not to mention his auntie, while old enough to be his grandmother, truly was a beautiful woman, though if he told her that, she'd probably beat him twice as hard next time they dueled.

They reached the staircase and descended, one slow step at a time.

"I keep forgetting to ask, what exactly are you an honored guest for?" Kamron said.

"Your guess is as good as mine."

Kamron snorted. Eventually they reached ground level, a few feet from a small dais where the queen and king sat adorned in splendid cream covered in silver, the candlelight flickering off the silver embroidery. Kamron smiled at his best friend's parents and bowed while Dess lowered to a curtsy.

King Corinne, Lukas's double but for age and eye color, smiled warmly at them and nodded his head. "Lady Dess, we are so happy you could join us, and are quite pleased to see your squire accompany you."

"Thank you, Your Majesty. I'm glad to be here, and the lad is quite a help on the road."

"I'm sure he is," the queen said. Her blue eyes sparkled with a joke, and she turned to Kamron. "Squire Kamron, I hope you enjoy yourself this evening and are a fair encouragement to our son."

Kamron wasn't sure what her words meant, but he nodded to her. "Encouragement with a healthy helping of competition is the bedrock of our relationship."

"I'm counting on it," the queen said.

Kamron narrowed his eyes at the queen, but a footman shuffled them to the side as another person was announced.

Kamron spied Lukas standing beside the dais and tried not to laugh at the cream and gold tunic he wore, matching his parents.

"Don't start," Lukas said, before turning to Dess. "Lady Dess, so good to see you again."

"You too, kid. Happy birthday," she said before rubbing his hair and messing it up. "Now if you'll excuse me, I'm going to go find some other old people I recognize." She threw Kamron a pointed look. "Behave."

"Yes, Auntie Dess."

She pinched Kamron's cheek and sauntered off into the crowd.

"Well, she seems to have forgiven you," Lukas said.

"Yeah, she was a little stiff at first, but after I told her my parents hadn't written, it was like she felt I'd been punished enough."

Lukas shook his head. "I can't imagine what my parents would do if they found out."

While they spoke, the announcer continued to list off titles and names in the background, until one title caught Kamron's attention. Lukas too straightened his posture as his eyes wandered to the balcony.

"Presenting Princess Briony of Hivagora, Ambassador for the Elvman."

A lovely woman in a flowing yellow gown crossed the balcony and paused for a dramatic moment at the top of the steps. She looked five or so years older than Kamron and Lukas and had bright forest-green swirls that wound over her exposed brown flesh in an elegant yet alien way.

Kamron had only ever seen Elv in tales, telepathic stories, and memories passed from person to person through time. Seeing an Elv now in person, he could barely believe it, but there were her swirls and her pointed ears poking through the braids of her updo.

"Wait, Briony, isn't that—"

"Yes. Yes it is," Lukas said.

The Elv princess descended the stairs into the nearly silent great hall. All eyes focused on her as stopped in front of the king and queen. She nodded respectfully, but did not bow or curtsey, exactly as she had in the tale Lukas's father told them of their first meeting long before Lukas was born.

After paying her respects to the king and queen, the princess moved past Kamron's and Lukas's spot beside the dais, her eyes pausing on Lukas for the briefest of moments before she moved into the crowd.

"When did she get here?" Kamron asked, still shocked at the preternatural figure from his childhood suddenly come to life.

"A week ago. She wandered out of the forest and said she'd come to fulfill her promise."

"Did she know it was your birthday?"

Lukas shook his head.

The story King Corinne told of Briony and her sister, one of the Misplaced like Kamron's mother, included him extracting a promise from the princess to return someday after reuniting her family, with hopes for diplomacy between their people. Apparently the Elv had waited quite a few decades to return her promise.

As the crowd returned to previous conversations, the king and queen stepped down from the dais to mingle, and music picked up as couples danced.

Unfortunately, the king spotted Kamron and Lukas lurking in the corner. He whispered something to his wife before breaking away. "Boys, remember, this party is a celebration. Stop looking so glum."

"Is there a way to get them to stop looking at us like we're a platter of sweetmeats?" Lukas asked.

The king watched as a small pack of mamas walked by with young daughters, eyeing the two boys with narrowed eyes. "Mm, I don't think that's likely. But maybe if you give a few of them your attention, it will stop the more passionate from trying to take a bite." The boys looked at the king as if he had two heads, and the king laughed and clasped them on their shoulders. "Now I know both of you have had plenty of decorum lessons and can be quite charming when you put your minds to it. So . . ." The king gestured between them.

Kamron frowned, not sure what he meant.

The king slumped in his silver finery and shook his head. "So put your mind to it. Dance with someone or I won't let you leave this room." The king gave them both pointed looks and walked away.

Lukas sighed and watched someone in the crowd to their left.

Kamron nudged his friend. "Come on, birthday boy. You first."

Lukas focused on his friend. “Okay, but I need your help.”

Kamron grinned. “Now that’s more like it. Tell me what you need.”

“Go eat one of those little quiches.”

“What?”

“Just do it, okay?”

Kamron rolled his eyes and stalked off to a nearby long table covered in treats. He picked up a small plate and began filling it with cheese and meats. He spotted the tray of quiche a bit farther down but wanted to be ornery and ignore his friend’s odd request. But . . . was that bacon on top of the little egg tart? He reached for the half empty tray and almost grazed knuckles with a green striped hand. He took a quick step back and bowed. “Excuse me, Princess Briony. I didn’t mean to be so rude.”

The princess raised one eyebrow. “Have you had one yet?”

“Not yet, my lady.”

“Then I insist you have one first.”

Kamron eyed her suspiciously. “This isn’t some ploy to poison me, is it? Because my mum taught me to detect most poisons.”

“I guess you’ll just have to find out.”

Kamron picked up one of the small tarts and popped it in his mouth, without checking it with his magic. It was delicious, and he nearly said so, before swallowing.

“Good, right?” the princess said, her face opening up with good humor. “I’ve had twelve,” she said with a grin.

Kamron grinned back and reached for another, but Briony caught up his arm, turning it over so his birthmark was visible. She ran her thumb over the mark in a way that was overly familiar.

“So odd. I’ve heard tales of this mark my whole life, yet I can’t feel a spark of magic in it.”

“Nor I,” Kamron said. And he had tried. With his unique unraveling magic, he thought for sure if anyone could, he would be able to undo the magic cursing his family.

Briony dropped his arm. “Sorry, that was probably improper.” She smiled again. “The Hu are quite concerned with such things.”

“And the Elv are not?”

She shrugged and grabbed another tart, popping it in her mouth while she leaned against the table. She gestured to a marble column a short distance away. It was carved into the shape of a large tree, stretching all the way to the ceiling, where the branches stretched out into arches, interconnecting with the other columns and holding up the ceiling and stained-glass windows. “Did you know this castle was created by Elv?”

Kamron grinned and crossed his arms. He liked this woman. “I did, actually. The king used to tell me and Lu stories when we were boys. Once he told us a story about how two Elv Princesses lit up this very room with the light of their beauty.”

The princess grinned. “He did not say that,” she accused, but before Kamron could reply, Lukas appeared.

“Ah, Kam, there you are,” he said, clapping his friend on his back.

“Lukas, you should try the quiche.” He gestured to the platter, but Lukas wasn’t listening and had turned to the princess.

“Lady Briony. It’s a pleasure to see you again.” Lukas bowed low, and when Briony didn’t reply, he continued. “Would you honor me with the next dance?”

Briony looked Lukas over, down and up again, and then her eyes stopped on his face. “No,” she said, and snatched another quiche before wandering off.

Lukas stood there for a long moment, and Kamron covered his mouth to hide his grin.

“Don’t say it,” Lukas said.

“Was that really your plan?” Kamron asked with a laugh.

Lukas sighed. “I thought maybe if she spoke to you first, she wouldn’t leave as quickly this time.”

“Wait, you’ve tried this before?”

"Three times. She arrived a few days ago, and I can't get more than a word from her."

"Really? She seemed quite nice. And funny."

"I know. I've heard her talk to other people."

Kamron laughed, but stopped abruptly when Lukas glared at him. "Sorry. It's your birthday, I can mock you tomorrow."

"Thank you. Besides, it's your turn now."

Kamron groaned and popped another quiche into his mouth. The whole thing felt pointless. He knew getting married and producing heirs was necessary, but he knew love like his parents had was rare, and he didn't think that sort of life was for him. It was too dangerous. He liked the safe, boring, and monotonous lifestyle much better.

Peering over Lukas's shoulder, he could see two girls standing near a tall flower arrangement. One wide and blonde, the other thin and brunette. The blonde had her back to Kamron as she chatted with the brunette. His eyes connected with the brunette over her friend's shoulder.

Sure, why not.

He turned back to Lukas. "I haven't been introduced to anyone," Kamron said.

"What?" Lukas asked.

Kamron sighed. "Introduce me to those two over there so I can dance with one. You could ask the other."

Lukas turned to look. "Which one do you want to dance with?"

"I don't care. The brunette works."

Lukas grinned. "Come on, then." Lukas led him to the two girls, and Kamron got a better look at the brunette as he approached. She was about his age, with a light brown complexion and pretty amber eyes. She was well styled but her dress didn't fit her shoulders right. "Lady Alis, may I make my friend Prince Kamron of Aluna known to you? Kam, this is Lady Alis of Qosha, and this is Lady Siblina of Eplaria. Both are studying at the Magical University of Pundica."

As soon as Lady Alis was introduced, Kamron bowed deeply to the lady and nodded to her friend. "Lady Alis, may I have your hand in the next dance?"

The lady smiled sweetly. "You may, Your Highness."

"Lady Siblina, may I have your next dance as well?" Lukas asked, and Kamron turned to look at the other lady for the first time. When his eyes landed on her round face, the world seemed to stop turning.

Her eyes shown the same blue as the summer sky at twilight, and her hair wasn't blonde, but golden and radiant, enhanced by the peach gown flowing over her full-bodied figure. She was absolutely beautiful. Their eyes connected. Her pink lips parted as if in surprise and her eyes twinkled. Then all at once her face closed off into a polite mask, and she turned to Lukas, offering a small curtsy.

"I would be honored to dance with you, Prince Lukas."

Her voice was clear, and sweet to Kamron's ears, yet it made his stomach turn. She should be saying that to him, not to Lukas. Kamron blinked and remembered who he'd asked to dance. He looked back at Lady Alis, who grinned at him.

The notes of the next song strummed from the orchestra, and Lady Alis raised her eyebrows. "Shall we?"

"Right." Kamron offered her his arm and tried not to look angry when Siblina took Lukas's. He danced with his partner, trying to be the genteel prince he'd been brought up to be, yet his eyes kept straying to the woman in his best friend's arms.

Lady Alis didn't seem to mind and was a good sport about the whole thing. "She's not attached," Lady Alis said, as Kamron's eyes strayed again when they entered a spin.

"Excuse me?" Kamron asked, his mind far away, bathing in blue orbs.

"Siblina. She doesn't have a beau. I just thought you might like to know."

Kamron smiled and returned his attention to Alis. "I'm sorry. I'm being very rude."

"I don't mind. I do have a beau, actually, but they're back at the academy. And they don't enjoy dancing very much."

"Then I'm honored to offer you a dance in their absence," he said, and meant it, liking the girl more and more by the moment. He tried to focus a little more on her for the remainder of the dance, but was relieved when it was over. He went with Lukas to fetch the two ladies' drinks. "Let me give one to Siblina, okay?"

Lukas snorted. "I had a feeling you'd say that. But won't Alis be put off?"

"Nope. We have an understanding."

Lukas chuckled but didn't argue when they returned to the ladies, and Kamron offered a glass to Lady Siblina.

"Lady Siblina, could I have the next dance?" Kamron asked, slightly out of breath for no reason.

Siblina turned to him, a sly grin on her face. "Oh, my. I didn't think you were much of a dancer, Prince Kamron."

"Why not?" What was she implying? Hadn't he danced well with her friend? He hadn't expected anything but her ready acceptance. Anything else would be considered rude.

"Well, it's just that you've only danced once in the last half hour and there are so many partnerless ladies. I feel, Prince Kamron, as if I might be taking an opportunity from one of them, dancing twice in a row."

"Please, call me Kamron."

"Of course, Prince Kamron."

Kamron frowned. He wasn't sure if she was uninterested or just being polite. "Perhaps I could have the dance after next?"

"I'm not sure. I'm not the best at seeing the future," she said again, with a little smile this time. Lady Alis snorted, and Kamron felt like he was missing a joke, likely at his expense.

"I will have to ask again later," Kamron said, with a bow that

Siblina returned. He and Lukas excused themselves, and Kamron spotted another lady to dance the next song with. If Siblina was serious about not wanting to take the spotlight, he would have to diversify.

Through the night, he danced every song with a new lady, forcing Lukas, to the delight of the king and queen, to do the same. He worked hard to keep his focus on his partner, but his eyes drifted far too often to Lady Siblina, and he was relieved at the few times their glances connected.

He asked her several times to dance, but each time she had an excuse, saying things like "I'm afraid I've had one too many of those delicious quiches, and the spinning might upset me," and "My left pinky toe is feeling a little funny and I wouldn't want to throw off the steps." Each denial was said with a little smile that made Kamron want to go mad, and didn't feel like a hard no. He didn't know what to make of this amazing and contrary girl.

That night he lay in bed with the moonlight glinting down on his face through a high window, and he thought of Siblina. He thought of every glance, every expression, and every word she'd spoken, and he analyzed their meaning. He needed to know her mind, to understand her person. It wasn't want, he told himself over and over as he lay awake long into the night. He didn't *want* to know her. She was a curiosity, nothing more.

But as the night grew long, fear and doubt crept in and he scratched subconsciously at the albatross on his arm. He wouldn't allow himself to want her. He would get to know her, learn her mind to satiate his curiosity, and then he could put her out of his mind and focus on more important things.

The next morning, he rose early and wandered into the breakfast hall where a buffet was laid out on one wall, and guests could come and go as needed. There were a few guests drinking tea or eating eggs, but not any he recognized. He left and did a lap around the castle gardens before returning. The brisk early winter air helped to clear his head. He needed to get a hold of himself. The night before he'd felt a lot of things he'd never felt before, and one of them was want. When the morning sun cast its light on his ceiling, he couldn't deny it any longer. He wanted Siblina, in so many ways. He wanted to know her thoughts, he wanted to see her laugh, and to learn what all her little expressions meant.

And that was bad.

Once through the gardens, he returned to the breakfast hall, which was now a bit fuller. There were a few lords he recognized and a few girls who'd giggled when he walked by. He sighed and wandered back upstairs. Dess was still sleeping, taking advantage of a no schedule day as thick curtains blocked out the eastern facing windows.

Kamron sat on a chair, his knee bouncing as he counted in his head. He'd reached three thousand five hundred and twelve before the impatience became too much and he set off again back into the breakfast hall. He scanned the crowd until he spotted the back of a perfect, golden head and his stomach did a little flip.

He took a deep breath and snatched up a plate from the side table, and loaded it with breakfast things, not paying attention to what he grabbed before wandering, seemingly at random.

"Ah, Lady Siblina, a pleasure to run into you this morning," he said, bowing to the radiant goddess, who wore pastel blue that brought out the azure in her eyes. Kamron pinched himself discreetly. Thoughts like that weren't productive. "And this lovely figure must be your mother," he nodded to the woman sitting next to Siblina.

"My aunt," Siblina said with a little grin. "Prince Kamron, may I make my aunt, Lady Filipa of Lasor, known to you? Aunt, this is Prince Kamron of Aluna, we met last night before he asked Alis to dance."

The aunt, whose eyebrows rose dramatically when his title was mentioned, gained a little smirk that matched Siblina's. "It is a pleasure to meet you, Your Highness."

She offered her hand, and Kamron took it, bowing. "The pleasure is mine, and you must call me Kamron."

"That's very generous of you. Have you been in Arnav long?"

"No, I arrived with my knight commander only a few hours before the party. But I've spent much time in the castle."

"Ah yes. I'd heard you and Prince Lukas were particular friends."

Kamron smiled warmly. "Yes, we've known each other since we were quite young, so this castle is as familiar to me as my own home. In fact, I happen to be excellent at giving tours." Kamron turned to the lovely figure, studying him. "Lady Siblina, have you seen the gardens?"

"Yes, I have," she said, her expression even and pleasant, not giving away a thing.

"Would you like to see them again?"

"What for?" She tilted her head as if curious.

Kamron blinked, utterly at a loss for words.

"Darling, will you please gather me a few sprigs of lavender from the garden?" Siblina's aunt asked. "I feel a bit down this morning, and I think the scent might liven things up."

Siblina's eyes flicked up, and a little crease appeared in the middle of her forehead. "The lavender is all dead this time of year, Aunt Filipa."

"But I believe the kitchen staff keep some rosemary in pots, and it has a most invigorating fragrance," Kamron said. "I would be happy to escort your niece to collect some for you, my lady."

"Oh, that would be quite lovely, thank you, Your Highness," Lady Filipa said with a small grin that Kamron recognized.

Lady Siblina watched him closely. He could not read her expression, but she took his arm when he offered it. They walked from the room as his mind churned over what she was thinking. He was used to women being direct and clear when they were annoyed with him or didn't want him around, and while Siblina wasn't eager, he also didn't feel like she wanted him to go away. It was like she was playing a game, but that didn't make any sense.

He led her down a long corridor toward the kitchens in silence.

He wondered how she would react if they went through the servants' rooms. Some of the upper class found the sight of others working undignified, but Kamron didn't usually associate with those sorts.

"Keep your fingers away from my sweets, you!" the kitchen chef said to Kamron, greeting him in her usual way.

"It's good to see you too, Maria," Kamron said, and gave the older woman a hug. "This is Siblina."

Siblina curtsied. "You wouldn't happen to have been the one behind those amazing quiches, were you?"

Maria's typically stern expression melted into one of joy. "I was indeed. They are a closely guarded secret I use to maintain job security."

"Well, it's definitely working." Siblina grinned.

A kitchen boy dropped a heavy tray into the sink, splashing a few other workers, and the food they were preparing, and Maria waved Kamron off while she handled the situation. Kamron grabbed Siblina's hand in the commotion and pulled her out of a side door into a small garden. The air was crisp in the early afternoon, yet the plants thrived. Siblina wandered toward the low stone wall. Her eyes fluttered from side to side as she glided between the buckets of herbs. She bent down, muttering to herself. Kamron couldn't watch from a distance any longer. He knelt beside her.

"Is it the pots?" Siblina asked.

Kam lifted one for her. "It's the brick under it." He pointed to the gray bricks sunk into the eres and covered with dirt and bits of decomposing leaves.

Siblina reached down and felt it. "It doesn't feel warm."

"The spells on the stone are very targeted. They don't heat the air or anything around them, only the eres in the pots. Not enough to grow most things out of season, just keep it alive and producing through winter."

"Right." Siblina nodded, and her forehead scrunched as she

thought through the spell work. "There's no need to fake the season completely, we have greenhouses for that. But this is enough to provide a kitchen with what they need. It's genius. And practical. I love when magic is practical and not showy, like the magic people at the university prefer."

Siblina grinned while she spoke, but then straightened, as if remembering he was there, and shook out her skirts.

"Do you like the university? You must be a hit, being able to detect magic so well. Most don't even notice it in this garden."

He wanted to know everything about this amazing woman. But it wasn't right, he shouldn't want it. He needed to get a grip.

"I've only been there three months. It seems too short a time for a snap judgment." Siblina shrugged and looked around. "So do you even know what rosemary looks like? Because I don't."

Kamron grinned at her. "You don't? How is that possible? Shouldn't you be learning all about that right now?"

"Three months, remember?"

"Right. Well, it's over here." Kamron stepped over to a big, bushy shrub and picked a sprig off the end. He held it out to Siblina, and she leaned in and inhaled, her chest rising and falling slowly.

Kamron looked away to clear his head. Siblina took the sprig, keeping it close to her nose. "And how do you know what it looks like?"

"My mum, she's a plant witch." A witch was the lowest of the accredited magical rankings, one not requiring a mage to attend the university. His mother had grown up under the eye of Wizard Gediminas. One of the few living mages with a wizard ranking. Gedas was an odd character, and sort of like another uncle. He would show up every few years and teach Kamron something interesting or throw a complex spell at him to unravel, then disappear for a while.

"Maybe I should get her to tutor me. I'm terrible at identification."

"Or I could, if you'll permit me to write you."

"Why would you want to write me?"

He shouldn't. He wanted to so badly, but he knew he should just end things here. Let her go back to school and let this be the end of knowing her. But he couldn't do it. He scratched at the birthmark on his arm.

"Because you're the most interesting person I've met in a very long time, and letting you leave without an assurance we will talk again would ruin me."

Siblina let out a little nervous laugh and turned around. "I can't believe you're real."

"I understand the sentiment." He circled her until he could see her face again. She grinned but wouldn't meet his eyes. He took her hand and raised it to his face, not yet sure if he would kiss it. Her eyes met his at last, and a spark shot into his very core. "Is that a yes?"

Before she could answer, a kitchen boy entered the garden and froze at the sight of them. They apologized and Kamron led her back through the castle to the breakfast hall, where he abandoned her with her aunt and fled back to the rooms he shared with Dess. His chest felt ready to burst, and he was desperate to get his head back on his shoulders.

"There you are. Pack our bags, laddie. We need to head out if we want to beat the traffic," Dess said, tossing a pack at him.

She was dressed, boots and sword belt on, as if ready to walk out the door. He didn't know what to do, frozen in shock as the pack hit him and fell to the floor.

"What's wrong?" she asked.

"I thought we might stay longer," he said at last.

"Yes, I'd hoped for a proper holiday, but Commander Rightwitch orbed me this morning that activity has picked up on the border. We need to go before war breaks out."

Kamron blinked and looked at the door. He needed to say goodbye to Siblina. He didn't owe her anything, but he needed it.

"You can call a servant to send for Lukas for your goodbyes, and have them ready our mounts to leave by the end of the hour."

"No, it's just . . ." But how did Kamron tell his auntie he wanted to say goodbye to a girl? He could have said it to Lukas, but his auntie would smile and tease him.

"Out with it, lad."

"I had someone else I wanted to tell."

Dess frowned at him and then her eyebrows went up and she smiled sickeningly sweetly. "Is it a girl?"

Kamron sighed and turned away from her, rubbing a hand over his hair.

Dess cackled. "Fine. But tell a servant to have our horses readied for us before the end of the hour."

Kamron nodded and ran from the room without another word. He raced down the hall and two flights of stairs to the breakfast room, pausing outside of it so that he might not be totally out of breath, but as he looked around the hall. He didn't see Siblina.

"Who are you looking for? Your best friend?"

Kamron looked down to see the much shorter Elv Princess, Briony, munching on a scone and standing away from the rest of the guests.

"Uh, no, I was looking for a lady. Forgive me, Princess Briony. It's good to see you this morning."

Briony grinned. "Don't worry about me. Who is it you're looking for? Now I'm invested. Is it the lady you danced with last night or the friend you couldn't keep your eyes off?"

Kamron stared at her, but she only grinned and munched on her scone. He signed. "The friend."

Briony nodded. "I thought so."

"So are you genuinely trying to throw Lukas off, or is there something you don't like about him?" Kamron asked. It was a bold question, but he felt like this woman wouldn't be offended. She was too observant not to see Lukas was trying to make himself known to her.

Briony sighed. "He's so young. I like his spirit, but he's young and I am not. I don't want to break him." She looked off down the hall. "Perhaps I should head back to my people and try this diplomacy in another decade or two."

Kamron shrugged. He needed to head off, but he enjoyed talking to the Elvwoman. He knew the Elv lived centuries longer than Hu, and Briony looked the same as she had when Lukas's father was young. "There will always be complications with diplomacy. But Lukas has a good head on his shoulder. Better than mine, honestly. Just make your opinions and feelings known. He won't break at a little rejection. Besides, it's the not knowing where you stand with someone that makes things the hardest."

Briony eyed Kamron carefully. "Such as with you and your lady?"

"Exactly."

"Well, I can help with that. She's staying on the second floor, third door down on the right."

Kamron blinked and then turned and took three big steps out of the hall, before pausing and returning to Briony. He took her hand and bowed over it. "My lady, it has been a pleasure to know you. My duties call me away this morning, but I hope for the chance to see you again if you stay in Arnav."

Briony smiled. "I hope for the same. Now go find your lady."

Kamron did just that. He counted off doors on the second floor, then paused outside what he hoped was the right one, straightening his tunic and collecting his thoughts. He knocked, and Lady Siblina answered.

"My lady, pardon my boldness, but my knight master has informed me we are leaving the city before noon. Please, do I have your permission to write to you? I will not do so if you do not wish it."

"Would you really?" Siblina asked, tilting her head to one side.

Kamron blinked. "Would I write to you?"

"No, would you really not write if I said I didn't want you to?"

Kamron thought about it, but shook his head. “I might write, but I wouldn’t send it. Instead, I would hope every day that our paths might cross again in the future, and that you might look on me more favorably then.”

Siblina looked down, her lips turning up in that funny little grin that made Kamron very aware of his heart beating in his chest. At last she met his eyes again, her face placid and polite. “You may write me at the university, though I cannot promise I will reply.”

Kamron’s stomach cartwheeled, and he stopped himself from doing a fist pump. Instead, he bowed gracefully. “I will write very excellent letters then, so as I might persuade you to reply.”

She curtsied, and he forced his legs to carry him back to the staircase to track down a servant before packing for their return to Aluna.

# Chapter Seven

"Gonna be the death of me, he is," Bruno muttered as he paced back and forth in Kamron's room.

"Look, Bruno. The plan is simple. Arnav's celebration is always held before noon, and ours is always after sunset. That gives me five hours leeway, easy."

"With all due respect, my lord, you are the biggest loon bird I've ever met," Bruno said, more seriously than Kamron had ever seen him.

Kamron grinned and tapped the albatross birthmark on his arm. "At least I come by it honestly." Kamron grabbed his fur-lined cloak and threw it over his shoulders before adjusting the hood in the mirror. He rubbed his chin, and the few stubbly hairs growing there. "Just tell anyone who knocks that I'm meditating before the celebration."

"An' what if your parents come knocking?" Bruno took Kamron's gloves off the dressing table and threw them at the prince's face, who caught them with ease.

Kamron's carefree air and grin melted. "Don't worry. They won't." He opened the door and left his rooms as quickly and quietly as possible.

Though the corridors were dark and empty, Kamron knew a castle never slept. The kitchens would be alight with the fires of the ovens, and there would be many sets of arms kneading dough in preparation for the feast that evening, that Kamron could not miss. He quickened his pace, walking on the balls of his feet in the silent manner his father had taught him.

Kamron had been in Tate, the new capital of Aluna, for three days, sleeping in the same castle as his parents, and they hadn't called for him or come to see him.

He also hadn't burst his way into their rooms as he would have before the fire two and a half years before, but that was because he feared he wouldn't be welcomed.

He slipped into the stables and readied Lightning for their midnight ride, thankful for the full moon to guide them. Kamron trusted Lightning, and while riding in the dark could be very foolish, he knew the road between Tate and Arnav well. He would be at the castle in the early morning and could nap, then slip into his best friend's knighting ceremony.

He hadn't been able to sleep, knowing the next evening he would come face-to-face with his parents whether he was ready or not, so he took to the road for a little fun before the stress of the next day. He needed it.

The last few months had been stressful enough: Vasniydor escalated their unofficial war, attacking and destroying an Alunan settlement, and Dess refused to return to the capital and lead from afar after her accident. Kamron had to step up significantly in his role, taking on much of the command, and frankly, he'd been surprised his parents hadn't sent someone to replace Dess and demand her return.

But all that was behind him now. He would see his best friend in a few hours and could relax a little. After tomorrow, he would get his orders and see what the future had in store. There was no use dwelling on it now.

When he at last reached the castle, he was dead on his feet as the adrenaline of the night cooled to exhaustion. A very surprised footman led him to a spare room, and he asked them not to notify the prince of his arrival and to wake him in time for the ceremony. The footman had to knock quite loudly before Kamron woke a few hours later and shouted at him to get lost. The timid man nervously entered Kamron's room and reminded him of the ceremony, which caused Kamron to leap from bed and ready as quickly as he could, after tipping the footman well.

The great hall of the Arnav castle was covered in flowers as nobles and dignitaries filed their way in. Kamron found a spot in the front of the crowd where he could duck behind someone tall so Lukas didn't see him.

As he waited for the ceremony to start, he scanned the crowd.

"Who are you looking for?"

Kamron turned and grinned as a lovely lady with green spirals covering her exposed skin squeezed into an empty spot beside him. "Princess Briony, it's good to see you. Would you believe me if I said I was looking for you?"

"Not at all."

"Well, it is good to see you either way. I'm glad you didn't return to the forest." Kamron spied a head of golden hair and rose on the balls of his feet for a better look. Disappointed, he glanced back at Briony.

"As am I. So tell me, who are you looking for?" Her grin grew a knowing look, and Kamron rolled his eyes.

"I was hoping I might find someone familiar in the crowd." There was another blonde a short distance away with her back to Kamron, but the color was off, more white gold than morning sunlight, and she was too skinny.

"Not a special lady, is it? Did you not keep in touch?"

"I did." Kamron smiled, then worried he looked like a fool, and stopped. "She said she might be here today."

He and Siblina had kept very much in touch. It started with him sending her letters full of facts and clippings of plants he knew well, repeating things his mother had told him often, but in each letter he made sure to ask her a question. Something simple or leading that would encourage a response. Siblina answered his letters with questions or thoughts on each plant and then would answer his personal question, revealing more and more of herself, her intelligence and humor. She always ended each letter with a postscript, thanking him for his plant knowledge and warning him that he could reply if he wished it, but she might be too busy in the future to return a reply.

She always replied, and Kamron always grinned at the postscript. It became a fond part of her letters, her pointed reluctance in conversing that always followed her open and honest correspondence. Over time, they stopped talking about plants and each letter was filled with stories or moments from their days, and they asked deeper and deeper questions. On the second anniversary of the Tross fire, Kamron told her of his past wrongs and his deep regret and shame. He told her about his parents' disgust and their absence over the years. He thought for sure it would be the first letter she didn't reply to, confident she would want to end their correspondence. But to his relief and delight, she replied. It was the first letter without a threat of no reply.

Two years of correspondence was maddening. He was desperate to see her again.

"Ah, that makes sense." Briony nodded and looked toward the stage as a footman came out with a pillow, placing it in the middle of the platform. "I didn't think you would be able to make it, given the day's times tables."

Kamron grimaced and glanced at the sun through the high stained-glass windows but was saved a reply as the king and queen entered and all present bowed as one. They stood behind the pillow and the king pulled a sword from his belt as a column of squires entered and lined up beside the dais. Lukas was the very last in line, standing tall and regal. Kamron smiled and ducked behind the tall man next to him. Briony snorted beside him.

"Squire Alice, approach and kneel," King Corinne said, his voice reverberating through the great hall.

The first squire in line, a tall woman with auburn hair and light brown skin, stepped forward and knelt on the pillow. The king tapped her shoulders gently with the heavy sword, and Kamron's stomach did a little uncomfortable flip. His heart rate picked up as the new knight rose and crossed to the other side of the platform, the crowd cheering, then dying down again as the next name was called. Kamron watched it all with glazed eyes. He'd attended plenty of knightings in his life. Ever since he was a small boy, watching the new knights cross the stage, Kamron dreamed about the day he would do the same. But now the thought shot pangs of anxiety through his chest. He wasn't ready. He wasn't noble enough. He hadn't done anything deserving of the honor, let alone to expunge his past wrongs.

His heart raced in his chest and he was ready to run from the room, for what reason he wasn't sure. Briony's hands gripped his arm tight, and he zoned back in on the stage.

"Squire Lukas, come forward and kneel," the king said.

Kamron balled his feelings and emotions up in a tiny sphere and shoved them down deep where they wouldn't bother him. He stepped out behind the tall guy and grinned up at his best friend.

Lukas stepped onto the dais, his chin high, and glanced at the crowd. His jaw was tight with nerves as his eyes scanned the crowd before falling on Briony. His face relaxed for just a moment.

Yep, he was still obsessed with the older Elvwoman, despite his letters to the contrary. Kamron grinned and shook his head as Lukas's eyes traveled from Briony to her arms around another man's arm and then to Kamron's own face. Their eyes connected for a moment, and Kamron saw the surprise, joy, and incredulity flash over his face before he turned to his parents. He knelt and bowed his head, likely to hide his expression.

The king lifted his sword one last time and tapped Lukas on each shoulder as he spoke. Briony squeezed Kamron's arm hard enough he winced. "I, King Corinne, do hereby dub thee Sir Lukas of Rohap, knight of the realm. May your compassion and wisdom become a shining example to the people of our land."

Kamron whooped and cheered as Sir Lukas of Rohap rose and faced the crowd and bowed. Kamron wasn't the only person cheering, but he was the loudest, and as Lukas stood from his bow, he gave Kamron the subtlest look of happy annoyance before leaving the dais.

"Let us all be merry and celebrate our new knights as our country grows stronger," the king said, before sheathing his sword.

The crowd moved toward the refreshment tables, and Briony released her grip on his arm. He turned to her, but she was gone, as if she'd melted into the crowd.

A heavy hand came down on his shoulder.

"What are you doing here?" Lukas hissed, his eyes wide.

"I couldn't miss my best friend's knighting," Kamron said, and pulled Lukas into a hug, which his friend only just accepted before pulling away.

"Well, you're about to miss your own."

Kamron shrugged. "Would that be so bad?"

Lukas stared at him. "Yes. Yes, it would. Come on, man, let's get you a horse." He dragged Kamron from the room.

"But I didn't even get any snacks yet," Kamron said, eyeing a table filled with cheese and meats. His stomach rumbled.

"You should have thought about that earlier. Come on."

They reached the stables, and Lukas ordered the stable hands to bring them two saddles.

Kamron glanced at his friend. "Won't your parents be mad if you miss the festivities?"

Lukas shrugged. "This sounds like more fun," he said as he threw a saddle on a horse.

Lightning would be brought back to Tate after she had a decent rest, so for their trip back, Lukas picked two fast mounts. They were saddled, and the boys led them from the stables as Briony walked past, leading her own horse, already saddled. "I'm coming too."

Lukas stopped and stared as the princess mounted the horse, her flowing gossamer skirt parting to reveal loose pants as she settled in the saddle. She looked back at them. "Aren't we in a hurry?"

The two princes mounted up and set off down the road leading south, toward the castle, only a half day's ride away.

"How do you feel?" Kamron asked Lukas, as Briony rode ahead, as if ignoring them.

Lukas puffed out his chest and pulled his shoulders back. He held the stance for a long moment, then let out a deep breath and deflated. He smiled at Kamron. "Exactly the same, to be honest."

Kamron frowned. "It seems like there should be some monumental shift. Right now, I feel like some little boy trying on his father's sword belt. There's no way this night ends with me being a knight."

"But you will be."

Kamron shook his head. He wasn't so sure. "What makes someone worthy of the title? People always use that word or talk of our honor. If you and I can be knighted as we are, what honor does anyone really have?"

"I think it's all a trap, to be honest."

Kamron looked at his best friend, totally at a loss as to what he meant.

Lukas laughed. "I don't think there's anything different between us and knights like Dess and Stonewall, just time and experience. I think calling it an honor and saying we are worthy is all a trick to make us try harder. It becomes an honor when we keep trying."

Kamron frowned, trying to piece it together. "So you're saying it doesn't matter that I'm still a rotten person who's done nothing of value in his life? As long as I do my job as a knight, it will be enough?"

Lukas started to nod, but Briony brought her horse to a sudden stop, causing the two eighteen-year-olds to jerk their horses around her. Her horse kept walking when they drew even.

"Is this really how you two numbskulls reason things out?" Briony asked.

Kamron's cheeks warmed, thinking she'd heard their conversation.

"Do remember, we didn't invite you to this journey, my lady," Lukas said, but Briony ignored him and turned to Kamron.

"You truly think you've done nothing of value?" Briony asked.

Kamron thought about it for a moment, but he couldn't think past the closed door of his parents' sitting room. He nodded slowly.

Briony rolled her eyes. "In six months you made Tross prosperous while the bulk of its commerce moved to Tate, then you saved a troop of soldiers who were being held prisoner by the enemy, and killed one of Vasniydor's top generals in a one-on-one duel. I believe you then dragged the half dead knight commander of the army across enemy lines back to base camp and managed to save her leg with your knowledge of medicinal herbs, even though you lack any training as a healer. And if I understand correctly, you basically led the army for the next three months while the commander recovered. Who cares about a little fire after all of that?"

Kamron looked at Briony, letting his shock show on his face. He glanced at Lukas. "How does an Elv diplomat to Rohap know so much about Aluna's private military happenings?"

Lukas's cheeks reddened and he looked away.

"He reads me your letters when I'm bored," Briony said, examining her nails.

"Not the personal parts," Lukas said.

"You told her about Dess," Kamron said, and the memory of her lifeless body flashed through his mind. It was the scariest week of his life when her fever broke out, and they still hadn't crossed back into Aluna.

"Everyone knows about Dess and the general," Lukas said. "People talk about you like you're a war hero."

"It wasn't like that," Kamron said, shaking his head.

"Life and death never are," Briony said. "It's only full of glory after the blood and mud are washed away."

# Chapter Eight

"Let me have your reins. You go," Lukas said as they neared the castle doors of the new Alunan capital in Tate. Kamron threw Lukas his reins and ran for the steps of the castle. He wound through the corridors toward the backdoor of the throne room, nearly running into a wall along the way.

They were late.

He had on his squire uniform, as was proper for attending Lukas's ceremony, and wouldn't be out of the ordinary for attending his own, but usually one arrived at their own knighting clean and wrinkle free. Not with mud on their boots and horsehair covering every inch of them.

He reached the hall behind the throne room and groaned. It was empty, meaning all the squires had moved into the hall, but he didn't think he was so late that the ceremony was over. He slowly inched open the door.

"Rise Lady Hellen of Onan, Knight of Aluna." The audience cheered the new knight.

Kamron sagged with relief. There were two more squires to go. He opened the door a little further and slid through the gap. He stood straight and walked carefully until he stood behind the other squires at the side of the stage, several hundred people standing before them. Kamron turned his head subtly to see if anyone had noticed him, and his eyes connected with Dess, who stood off to the side in front of the squire line as Kamron's sponsor.

Kamron broke eye contact and faced front as if he hadn't just faced down a raging bochnid.

"Come forth, Squire Branson," King Silas said, and the squire in front of Kamron moved to the dais.

At the sound of his father's voice, for the first time in over two and a half years, Kamron's heart rate picked up again.

After their serious talk on the long ride south, Lukas and Briony had pulled him into jovial conversation, lightening the mood and taking his mind off what he rode toward. They hadn't ridden with any haste, and the importance and significance of the journey sunk to the background and he enjoyed the ride with his friends. He'd focused on fielding the conversation between Lukas and Briony as he tried to engage her, and she teased him. Then she switched to teasing Kamron, telling Lukas he wasn't really there for him, only for the Lady Siblina who might have attended. Lukas laughed and teased Kamron along with her. Kamron only rolled his eyes and rode ahead, glad his best friend and Briony were at last bonding over something.

"Squire Kamron, come forth," Queen Elodie said, and Kamron was suddenly back in the throne room, his heart threatening to pop out of his chest. His hands trembled, and he clasped them behind his back before stepping forward. He couldn't meet his parents' eyes as he knelt before them.

His mother raised a sword and lowered it to each of his shoulders, tapping gently, while his father spoke. "Rise Sir Kamron of Tross, Knight of Aluna. Your courage and intelligence will be a strength to this land."

Kamron rose, his head still bowed to his parents. The crowd behind him cheered, and he spoke softly only for their ears. "Thank you. I hope one day to be worthy of the honor."

"You already are, my son," Queen Elodie said, and Kamron looked up. His parents smiled down at him as one, their eyes filled with tears. He almost lost it, but he looked away and turned toward the crowd. The noise of the room reached through his emotions, and he spotted Briony and Lukas cheering and shouting. Then his eyes fell on the shining figure standing next to them and nothing else seemed to matter.

Their eyes connected and Lady Siblina grinned and gave a little wave. He felt on top of the world knowing she'd come all this way to celebrate him.

A hand fell on his shoulder, stopping him from leaving the stage, and his father stepped forward to address the crowd. "Thank you all for coming to celebrate our new knights. Eat and make merry with them long into the night as we commemorate their years of hard work."

The crowd began to break up, and Silas leaned in and whispered. "Come walk with me, Sir Kamron."

Kamron followed his parents into the empty hall behind the throne room. His mother handed the sword to his father, who sheathed it at his waist. Kamron didn't know where to look, didn't know what to say.

"Tell me, how have things been at the northeastern border?" Silas asked. Kamron met his green eyes and was surprised to see he was nearly on the same level with his father, just shy a few inches. His father had always been so much larger than life, and Kamron didn't think he would ever reach the same height.

He wasn't sure if his father expected a militaristic answer or something else. Dess sent back daily and weekly reports, so nothing he said would be a surprise.

"The situation is stable," Kamron said, looking up at the king not as his father but as his commander. That was easier. "Vasniydor remains publicly oblivious to the attacks and the forces battering our border towns seem more interested in hit-and-run tactics than in occupying our land. Vasniydor has made diplomatic gestures to apologize for the actions of their misguided general, and insists he was acting without their knowledge. They have sent some of their own troops to the border on the guise of helping us with our bandit problem."

"And what is your assessment?"

Kamron let out a slow breath. "Our spies in Vasniydor have told us for a long time that the king wishes to take the corner of our land that lies between Vasniydor and Oskela before launching a proper attack on Kelnan, but I believe this is subterfuge."

"And your reasoning?"

"If they planned for more, they would have done it by now."

"Does it change our approach?"

"No, but I believe it's important to keep in mind as we progress, and it might be worth sharing with Oskela so that they are aware."

"I agree. Make sure it is done."

"Sir?" Kamron asked. Was his father sending him back to the border under Dess or under a new knight commander?

"Your first command as a knight will be to take over for Dess. It will be announced tomorrow, but I thought you should know before then."

"But I'm only a first-year knight."

"Who has already taken on most of the command in the last year. Do you see someone else more qualified?"

Kamron shook his head. "Thank you, sir."

"You earned it. Dess hasn't been vague about the work you've done the last few years on the border, and the situation in Tross could have gone differently had you not been there to assist Celes."

"We do, however, have one request when you take the position," Elodie said, coming to her husband's side.

"Anything, Mum."

Elodie held out her hand, and Kamron took it. "We hope you don't follow in Dess's footsteps in believing you must live on the steps of every conflict. The commander of the Alunan Army has historically operated from the capital, and while you can always take trips when it's needed, we hope you'll stay closer to home. At least for now."

"But I thought you didn't want me here."

"We never wanted that," Silas said, putting his hand on Kamron's shoulder.

"We thought it would be best to distance ourselves, and it's been the hardest thing I've ever done," Elodie said, her voice breaking.

"I get it," Kamron said, looking down as heat built behind his eyes. "You spent fifteen years giving me everything I didn't deserve and then had to pack a lifetime of timeouts into a few short years. I deserved it. I didn't know what loss truly meant back then, because I'd lacked nothing, but I get it now."

His mom pulled him into a tight hug, and his father wrapped his big arms around both of them, squeezing them all into a tight family sandwich as he had through Kamron's youth. He felt home for the first time in a long time. He tried to subtly wipe his eyes when they broke apart, but it was useless. His dad cried openly as he leaned in and kissed his forehead. "I love you, son."

"I love you too, Dad."

"And I love you most!" Elodie said before kissing Kamron on the cheek.

"Ugh, I love you, but we need to cut it back a little, I think," Kamron said, wiping his cheek and forehead.

"That doesn't work," Elodie told him. "Kisses sink in and go straight to the bone, so you can never get rid of them."

Kamron stared at his mother, horrified for a moment, until his mom and dad both attacked him, kissing every inch they could reach. He beat them back, laughing until the door to the throne room opened.

"Really? Can't you three take anything seriously?" Dess asked.

Silas turned to her. "And can't you remember how to block a sword thrust? Or have you gotten too old?"

Dess punched Silas in the stomach, and he let her, not even

flinching when the blow connected. Kamron shook his head. He might be reaching him in height, but one of Dess's punches still took him out.

"Yep, definitely too old," Silas said with a grin, and opened the door to the throne room.

"How did that tonic work for your leg?" Elodie asked Dess.

"It did wonders. I didn't feel it all night," Dess told her.

"Wonderful. I'll make you some more tomorrow." She squeezed Dess's shoulder and followed Silas into the throne room.

Dess rolled her eyes to Kamron and walked a few paces, her new limp barely showing, till she was close enough to punch him, which she did.

Kamron flinched and gasped. "I'm sorry! If you don't want me taking over command for you, I'll tell Dad. Just don't hit me anymore."

Dess laughed. "Don't be a baby. I was the one to recommend you as my replacement. That was for being late. Where on eres did you need to go the day of your knighting?"

Kamron straightened and smoothed out his tunic. "I didn't go anywhere. I was in my room meditating and lost track of time."

"Mm hm, and Bruno is a great liar. Try again."

Kamron sighed and slumped against a wall. "It was nerves. I rode to Arnav to attend Lukas's knighting, so I didn't have to lie in bed wondering if Mum and Dad would skip me in the knighting ceremony and make me repeat the year."

Dess rubbed his head and turned back to the throne room. "You really need to worry less. Go get cleaned up and get your butt back to your party."

# Chapter Nine

"You should go dance with her."

Kamron blinked and glanced at his mom. She wasn't a quiet walker like his dad, so he must have been very oblivious for her to sneak up on him. He'd been standing by a pillar, watching Siblina talk with Lukas and Briony for the last few minutes, too nervous to approach.

"I shouldn't," he said.

"Why not?"

"Because it's not safe."

"What do you mean?" his mom asked, but then her expression morphed into a knowing look. "This isn't about your reluctance to *want* anything, is it?" She added a mocking lilt to the word "want."

"Mum, you're the one who told me what happens when our family wants. I don't understand why you're so insistent it doesn't matter."

His mother let out a slow, even breath. "I should have waited until you were older to tell you about our curse. But I knew about it from a young age, and keeping it secret felt wrong." She sighed. "Kamron, dear. It's not that you can't want for anything. I have so many things I want and have had and enjoyed in my life. I wanted your father, and I didn't let the spell stop me from being with him. I wanted . . . I wanted a child, and I didn't let the curse stop me from having you."

Kamron rolled his eyes. "Yes, but you only ever had one, and you waited an awfully long time to have me."

Pain and fear flashed in the queen's eyes before she closed them. "You're right. I have let the fear of our curse slow me down. But I regret it. You could have had an army of older siblings, but I let fear win."

Kamron shook his head. "No, it wouldn't have worked. I was born to be king," he grinned. "And if I had been born a few decades before, then Lukas and I wouldn't be friends like we are now."

"So everything happens in its time then," the queen said and kissed Kamron's cheek. "My point is, don't let fear keep you from the greatest things in the world. Love is so precious and should be captured whenever possible. The curse will come when it comes. Don't let it arrive and find whatever it takes is insignificant, because you never lived a meaningful life."

"So you're saying I should give it more things to take from me?" Kamron asked, raising an eyebrow.

"No, I'm saying you need to forget it. Don't let it hang over you like some looming dread. Gedas was always telling me the same about my future and I never listened. Live your life. Love your life. There was a saying back in the illusion that fits here." His mom grinned, and Kamron braced for whatever nonsense she was about to bring up from her time in another world. "Yolo."

He sighed. "What does that mean?"

"Yolo. You only live once." She patted his arm. "So go live."

Kamron took a deep breath and looked down at the mark on his forearm. He thought maybe it was easier for his mother, the mark of her curse was on her collarbone, so she didn't have to see it every time she reached for something. Perhaps she could even go an entire day without thinking about it. Kamron couldn't.

He turned from his mom, back to his friends, but they'd been swallowed by the crowd. Navigating through the celebrators, he accepted congratulations as he went, but Siblina wasn't where he'd last seen her. He growled and turned toward the stage, hoping a higher view would help him locate her.

And then there she was. A wraith in malachite satin, she crossed the room as if her feet barely touched the surface, like a hummingbird gently caressing a petal with her presence.

He shook himself. He didn't want to lose his head. It was his first time seeing her in two years, and while they'd grown to know each other well in letters, he couldn't be the well thought out correspondent in person. What if she thought he was a dork, or what if she was again the aloof lady who wanted nothing to do with him? But then she was before him, and he had to say something.

He bowed deeply. "Lady Siblina, I'm honored to see you again."

Siblina curtsied in one fluid motion. "Sir Kamron, congratulations on your achievement."

He couldn't read her expression. It drove him mad. He took a step forward, and she matched that step till he could reach out and touch her if he wanted—and he did want to.

"I'm so glad you came." He clasped his hands together to keep them from shaking.

"Surprise." Siblina grinned, and Kamron's heart melted.

He laughed, a weight lifting off his chest. "You said you were going to Lukas's ceremony."

Siblina's grin bloomed into a full smile, and her eyes sparkled. "And you rode there the night before your own ceremony."

Kamron bit his lips, but he didn't deny it. A few strums of a loot rung from the musicians, a warning call to those present. "Would you do me the honor of this dance?"

She could say no, she'd done it many times before. But she didn't. Instead, she held out her hand, and he took it, his flesh igniting where they connected. As he led her to the cleared space where other couples gathered, he caught sight of Lukas and Briony in the crowd making kissy faces and shaking their fists in celebration at Kamron. He flashed them a rude hand gesture before turning to Siblina, who grinned, but didn't look directly at him.

The music began, and they danced. Their eyes connected as their steps synced, and it was as if Kamron floated on the wings of his hummingbird.

He loved this woman with all his heart. He knew that now. She was everything he'd never wanted but could ever desire. They would be married. Not yet, but in a few years, after she graduated from the university, and one day they would have a family. Kamron knew it with every fiber of his being. Just as he knew he would do everything in his power to protect her and their children.

He wanted her. He wanted her children. He wanted to grow old with his family, and someday hold his grandchildren. The knowledge of that want terrified him, but he couldn't let it stop him from having it. That would only let the curse win, but in a different way.

By the time the song ended, Kamron was a changed man in a way that turning eighteen, killing the soldier who attacked Dess, and becoming a knight never could have changed him.

Kamron led Siblina from the dance to a table laden with iced fruit juice and handed her a glass. Lukas, followed closely by Briony, met them, and Lukas bowed to him.

"Sir Kamron, wonderful to see you, old chap."

Kamron adopted a stogy expression and bowed to Lukas. "Sir Lukas, how delightful to see you. How is your horse?"

"You two think you're quite funny, don't you?" Briony asked. Kamron and Lukas grinned and nodded.

They chatted for a bit before the musicians strummed again.

Lukas turned to Briony and bowed, extending his hand. "Princess Briony, would you honor me with this dance?"

Briony crossed her arms and glared at Lukas. Lukas's smile did not waver, nor did his hand, hanging in the open space before him.

Briony sighed and dropped her arms. "Fine. But you know my rule."

She took Lukas's hand and he pulled her to the dance. "Yes, yes, I know. I'm not allowed to fall in love with you." He winked at Kamron and sauntered off.

When they were out of sight, Kamron and Siblina broke into giggles.

"He's a goner," Siblina said.

Kamron nodded. "But at least he's going in with both eyes open."

Silence fell between them, and Kamron glanced at Siblina to see her watching him. A small smile on her lips.

"You spoke with your parents. How did it go?" she asked.

"I'm not sure. Better, but I think time will tell."

"Good. I know not being in touch weighed on you."

Kamron nodded. "They're giving me command of the Alunan Army."

"Really? Does Dess know?"

Kamron snorted. He'd told Siblina all about Dess and her lovingly firm hand with training. "Yes. She's decided to retire at last."

"So, does that mean you'll be headed back to the border?"

"Actually, my parents asked me to try leading from the capital. Dess only stayed in the field to avoid politics."

"And they want you to learn the ins and outs of the politics, no doubt," Siblina said, grinning.

Kamron grinned too. "Probably." Being in the capital also meant traveling from Tate to Pundica, and the magical university, was much quicker, and based on the way Siblina grinned at him, he suspected her thoughts were going to the same place.

"So what does the future hold for you?" he asked.

"Did I ever tell you of my family's magical legacy?"

"No, I believe you've excluded most of the interesting points in our correspondence."

Siblina glared at him. "Is that supposed to mean my letters are boring?"

"Absolutely not. They are the bright point of my life."

Siblina smiled up at him, and for that moment, his life was utterly perfect.

"Quite an entrance you made earlier," a voice said from behind Kamron, causing him to jump, but he didn't take his eyes off Siblina.

"If we ignore her, do you think she'll go away?"

Siblina shook her head at him before ducking around him.

"Since I don't think he's going to bother, I'll introduce myself. I'm Siblina."

"Iris." The two ladies nodded to each other. "I'm his second cousin. One of a dozen or so, but we're the only two of an age, so unfortunately we got lumped together as kids." Her eyes flicked to the dance floor where Lukas and Briony spun about, but then she looked back at Siblina, her smile almost looking genuine.

"That must have been miserable," Siblina said.

"Quite."

"Well, if you two are nice and cozy, I might as well excuse myself," Kamron said. To his delight, Siblina slipped her arm through his to keep him in place. He knew he was grinning like an idiot, but he didn't care.

# Chapter Ten

Down the hall from the kitchens, in a back corner of the Tate castle, was a small room, not much bigger than a closet, that had been assigned as an office for the knight commander of the Army.

Kamron was positive Dess had never set foot in this room. The move of the capital from Tross to Tate meant shoving two operating castles into the space of one, and while all the necessary operations had space to function, some of those spaces were less than ideal. The room was small, with a desk and two chairs. All available space was taken up by boxes crammed in on either side of the door, creating a small path. The boxes contained paperwork and maps, mostly. All things that a commander would need, wedged in with several decades of paper reports.

Being down the hall from the kitchens meant as Kamron worked on sorting recent reports, he was always hungry. Luckily, the head chef had known him since he was a boy, and he didn't need to say a word, only poke his head in the kitchen, and a sandwich or pastry appeared. All in all, it wasn't a terrible office.

Being the official knight commander was much less interesting than Kamron had imagined. He'd made solid relationships with the individual commanders and knights on the border, and they reported to him frequently, his communication orb glowing throughout the day. He took reports, studied maps, and tried to plan for the future.

The Twoshy was composed of fourteen countries who'd colonized the continent together, forming a treaty, the Constitution of Sixteen. Their constitution provided clear limits to their influence over each other, and their individual freedoms to coexist. As long as the constitution was upheld and intact, no country could wage war against another without the whole of the Twoshy rising against them.

Unfortunately, in the years surrounding the break of the spell that had held Kamron's mom captive, several of the countries had broken the constitution, rendering its protections void. Aluna, Vasniydor, and Oskela were all on that list. The consequences of this meant if any of these countries attacked another or were attacked, the rest of the Twoshy would not engage. It also meant that after centuries of these nations only having the most basic of militaries, training and arming their people became a new priority.

Aluna was a political and economic force in the Twoshy. It didn't make sense for Vasniydor to come for them, but Oskela was much more vulnerable. Its only protection was the small sliver of Aluna that protruded north, separating Oskela from a fully exposed border with Vasniydor.

This peninsula, as it was often thought of, was vulnerable and incredibly crucial for Vasniydor's offense, which is why the small villages of the peninsula were always under attack from bandits and raiders everyone knew belonged to Vasniydor.

Kamron considered their options. Holding the land was messy, and it wasn't particularly valuable while always under attack, but giving it up would be handing Oskela over on a silver platter to the enemy.

Not to mention Emperor Diego was another of the Misplaced, a victim of the crazed evil wizard like Queen Elodie. Kamron's mother would never forgive him if his strategy abandoned Oskela.

Kamron leaned back in his chair and stretched out his neck.

The potential war was a problem for Aluna's security, but it had been hanging for decades. Something else ran in the back of Kamron's mind, day in and day out, that felt like a greater vulnerability. Kamron believed the greatest threat to his life was the same one that had threatened his mother's. Far to the south, in a cave in the middle of the Tokke Mountains, was an old, crazed wizard who had wielded his magic and disrupted the political power for the entire continent.

Wizard Viclor, the man who'd imprisoned his mother and the other Misplaced in another world for over a century, was still alive and still capable of great evil.

Kamron wanted to build a life that was safe for Siblina, and somewhere deep in his heart, he knew Viclor was a threat. He thought about the problem for months as he studied maps in his small office. At night, he dreamed about it.

Problem was, he had no information about what went on in that cave in the mountains, and his mother made him promise when he was young to leave the wizard alone. Still, he needed eyes to watch and observe.

Kamron picked up the letter on the edge of his desk, and read over the messy writing, scrawled by a hand who was too busy for correspondence and drafted by a heart who wanted to write a hundred letters. Siblina was studying for exams, and the work was a strain. She didn't complain, but Kamron could tell, and he wished he could cheer her up.

Unable to sit any longer in his small windowless office, he gathered up his half-drafted letter to Siblina and tucked it and her message in his pocket. He set off through the halls of Tate to the largest suite of rooms in the castle, improbably on the first floor. For as long as Kamron had noticed such things, the castle security had been reluctantly accommodating to the king and queen's demands to keep their ground floor suite with its large patio doors opening up to a magnificent garden. It was walled in, of course, and the queen had designed the garden, planting protective plants in a way that beat the security of a tower fortress. Even so, it was the legendary complaint of their nation's vulnerability. Kings and queens did not sleep on the ground floor with their doors always open to a courtyard garden.

The suite and walled garden had been a one-year anniversary present from the king to the queen, and it was one of many reasons the royal family spent more time in Tate than Tross, long before any fires were set.

Without knocking, Kamron pushed open the doors to his parents' sitting room but paused at the open doors to the patio until his mother noticed him and gestured him forward.

She was bent over a fern and showed him the iridescent purple spores getting ready to spread from a rolled-up frond.

"What's this one do?" Kamron asked, knowing everything in his mother's garden had a use, if nothing more than being pretty.

"Believe it or not, I created this one for the pigment." Elodie rubbed a finger over the rolled-up frond and held out her hand. Kamron placed his brown hand in her pale white one, and Elodie ran her finger over the back of it, leaving a trail of iridescent shimmer. "I created an eyeshadow out of it for your auntie Kat back when we were a little older than you."

Kamron looked closely at the spores, and it gave him an idea. "Do you still have any of it?"

"I could whip up a batch." His mother eyed him carefully. "When do you need it by?"

"Well, that's what I came to talk about. I was thinking I might make a trip."

Elodie nodded and led him down a cobblestone path to a small clover-filled opening under a large, warped oak tree. Elodie moved the oak tree from Tross. As a child, Kamron marveled over the tree with a metal shackle grown into the trunk. The tree had a colorful past, but now it lived a simple life, currently casting shade onto a large, sleeping king stretched out on the clover below.

Elodie bent over the sleeping king and sketched an iridescent heart over his coal black forehead, before sitting next to him, her skirts flowing around her.

King Silas's soft snore didn't change as he grunted. "That better come off, eventually."

"Eventually," Elodie agreed and patted her husband on the chest.

Kamron found a soft spot on the clover and sat across from his parents as he waited for his dad to sit up and pull his wife half onto his lap.

These were the moments he'd missed in the few years of silence before his knighting. Before, he'd rolled his eyes at his parents' obvious affection, but now it made his chest ache for the opportunity to have what they had, and to enjoy it long into old age as they did.

Silas pulled his wife close for a moment and looked her squarely in the face. "Is my forehead glowing or going to sprout tendrils or some flower bud?"

Elodie bit her lips as she often did when trying not to laugh. "Nope."

"That's a relief." The king turned to his son. "How are you, Kam?"

"I've been thinking I should take a trip into the field."

Silas yawned and scooted himself and his wife on his lap till he leaned against the oak. That wasn't a good sign. He usually feigned disinterest, thinking it would lower Kamron's guard. And it probably would have, had Kamron not known his parents as well as they did him.

"Any particular field?" Elodie asked, her eyes open and innocent. "Perhaps one in Pundica?"

Kamron sighed and folded his legs underneath himself. "I could make a trip of it. Stop in on Pundica for a brief visit with our allies, then Oskela to talk with my counterpart there, and finally, down to the border with Vasniydor to spread morale and get a feel for how the situation has changed."

Silas and Elodie looked at each other, their expressions mirroring interest. "Visiting with allies, is that what the kids are calling it these days?" Silas asked.

Elodie made a sickening kissy face. "You are my greatest ally."

Kamron covered his face while his parents kissed and made retching sounds. "You two are too much. Honestly. Can't a body exist around you in peace?"

His parents burst into laughter and he waited, picking apart clovers until they finally got control of themselves.

"So can I go or not?" Kamron asked when their hysterics seemed to be coming to an end.

King Silas wiped tears of mirth from his eyes before addressing his son. "You don't need to ask our permission to see your girlfriend."

"She's not my—"

But Silas didn't let him interrupt. "You don't even need to ask our permission to go to Oskela or the border. You're your own man now, and you have your command. You do need to keep us informed, and we can obviously veto your plans, if we feel there is a mistake, but we aren't going to stop you from going to Pundica, to see your allies," Silas said, finishing with a grin.

Kamron's cheeks grew hot and he looked away. "Then I'm informing you of my plan to travel through Pundica and Oskela to the border and back. I should be back in two months or so."

"Take your time," the queen said with a slight grin.

Kamron glanced away again and looked up into the oak tree, where he couldn't see his parents' smirks. "Commander Joon will take over my clerical duties while I'm gone."

"I'll have that pigment ready for you in the morning. Stop by before you leave," Elodie said.

Kamron nodded. "I will. Thank you."

"Well, if that's all," the king said. "If you'll excuse us, I think a meeting of allies is needed."

Kamron fled the garden.

The road to Pundica was not overly eventful. The journey gave Kamron the chance to stop in Leronia briefly to see some of his cousins of the Misplaced family tree, but before long, he laid eyes on the two rivers that created an x in the center of the city of Pundica. On the northern bank sat an academic university, on the southern, the magical university. The western bank held the capital building where their elected council met and held business. The Eastern bank was left open as a public space, which frequently held celebrations or markets like the one Kamron rode through before crossing an old brick bridge and entering the grounds of the magical university.

Kamron knew what room number Siblina lived in, but not where it was located. He took a few wrong turns and asked directions from distracted looking mages who didn't need to pull their noses out of their books to point him in the right direction.

She wasn't in her bedroom, but her roommate directed him to the main office where she assisted with administrative work.

Kamron leaned against the desk outside of the office and cleared his throat, but the thin mage with his nose inches from an unrolled scroll didn't notice him. Kamron knocked on the desk. The mage blinked twice and glanced up before returning to his scroll.

"I'm looking for Learner Siblina."

The man pointed his thumb over his shoulder at the door. "She's inside."

Kamron nodded and reached for the doorknob.

The studying mage leapt to action too late. "Wait, you can't go in there!"

But Kamron was already through the door. Two women paused

their work and glanced at him. The first woman looked a decade or so older than himself, tall with straight black hair and bronze skin. The other was the love of his life. Her round face glowing with shock and delight.

"Kamron, what are you doing here?" she asked, her eyes flicking to the older woman with apprehension.

Kamron glanced at the older woman and bowed his head. "My apologies. I didn't mean to intrude. I came to escort Learner Siblina to lunch."

Siblina set down a notebook and stepped forward. "Kamron, may I introduce you to Wizard Adelina, head of the university."

Kamron's stomach sank as he realized his mistake of barging in on one of the most powerful people on the planet.

"Wizard Adelina, may I make known to you my particular friend, Sir Kamron of Aluna?"

Kamron noted when the wizard's eyes flicked to the birthmark on his arm, then back up to his face.

"Sir Knight," the wizard said. "Lady Siblina is one of my favorite pupils."

"She is mine as well," Kamron said, then floundered. "My favorite of your pupils, that is." Siblina covered her mouth and made a choking noise. Kamron put a hand on her shoulder and slowly backed toward the door. "I'll make sure she's well and bring her back fully fed."

"See that you do."

Kamron made it into the hallway, his hand still on Siblina's shoulder, and she closed the door, turning on him. "Really, it's not like she's a rabid animal."

"Yes, she is," the mage at the desk said.

Siblina rolled her eyes and shook her head at Kamron. "When did you get here?"

"Just now." He reached for her hand and she let him take it. He pulled her knuckles to his lips and kissed them gently. "Did you miss me?"

"Of course. Letters just aren't the same," Siblina said.

"Will you marry me?"

"What?"

He hadn't meant to blurt it out like that, but now he'd said it, he wasn't taking it back.

"After you graduate. Not now. I wouldn't want to take your accomplishments from you, but I can't stand waiting, at least for an answer. After you get your ranking, will you come live with me in Tate and never leave?"

"I wish you would both leave now, personally."

Kamron glanced at the mage studying at the desk, but he didn't look up. Siblina giggled and led him down a few halls till they reached a quiet corridor.

It was as if something relaxed in Siblina, something Kamron had never realized was tightened into a knot. She leaned into him, and her arms snaked up, wrapping around the back of his neck.

And Kamron only had to lean down for their lips to connect, sparks exploding where her plump lips met his. His hands found her hips and he wrapped his arms around her full figure, pulling her tight against him as he lifted her up and spun her around. Her kiss turned to giggles against his cheek, and he set her down gently. His eyes roamed every inch of her face, trying to memorize this moment and her exact expression, pure joy coating every feature.

They kissed for a while longer, then Siblina led Kamron into one of the university gardens where they wandered, enjoying each other's company.

"I knew on our first dance that you were the woman for me and that no other would ever do," Kamron told her.

"Really? On our first dance, you say?"

"As I spun you around the room and the light reflected in your eyes, I knew," Kamron said, confident in his decision.

"Romantic. Such a lovely picture you paint with your words."

"Not as lovely as the original."

"Oh dear. You flatter me too much. My head will get too big."

"Good, all the more head for me to love," he said, and leaned in to kiss her forehead, and her nose, and her lips. "How about you?" he asked when they broke apart.

"What?"

"When did you decide to marry me?" Kamron asked. "Was it really when I asked?"

Her lips parted into the smallest, most delicate grin, and his heart swelled. He loved that grin.

"I knew the moment I saw you. When you asked my friend to dance, and I swung about."

Kamron stopped, and Siblina walked a pace, before turning back. That little grin may not have been as innocent as he'd imagined. "The moment you saw me?" he asked.

"Yes." Her grin deepened.

"How very fanciful of you, to know with one glance who you should marry."

"Well, my grandmother did always say I have a sight of sorts," Siblina said, studying a nearby shrub.

"What do you mean?" Kamron asked.

Siblina laughed and kept walking. Kamron followed—how could he not follow the girl who'd stolen his heart?

"It's a gift from her line. She had a sister who passed young with the same gift. She said the site allowed one to see the right of things. Not always, but sometimes, when it really matters. When I turned and saw you in that ballroom, I knew. I knew there would never be anyone more right for me than you, and that one day we would marry."

Kamron shook his head. "You knew?"

"I knew."

"You knew the first time you ever saw me?" Kamron stopped again and stared at her. "Then why on eres did you reject my advances? If you knew I was right for you then, why did you put up such a fight?"

"Well, what fun would that have been?" Siblina asked with her little grin.

Kamron let out an offended gasp. "You strung me along for years, threatening not to reply to my letters for your own enjoyment?"

"Didn't you enjoy it as well?"

Kamron thought about that. "Well, yes."

"See? I'm always right. You should remember that for our marriage." She pointed a finger at him and he snatched it out of the air, pulling her closer until he could again wrap his arms around her.

"Yes, my love."

Kamron didn't know this woman quite as well as he had thought. But he was lucky. The intelligent, calculating, and playful woman she turned out to be was better than he could have ever imagined.

It was three years before Siblina earned her enchanter status at the university. Three hard years filled with lots of ink-stained fingers before Siblina learned the spells to make her own orb so they could talk long into the night. Kamron made many trips to Pundica, and sometimes continued on to the border to observe the ever changing, yet never progressing tension with Vasniydor.

# Chapter Eleven

"Never have I seen a person sweat so much," Lukas said, throwing a handkerchief at Kamron. Kamron wiped from his forehead down to his chin. "Maybe you should have worn black to hide the flop sweat."

"Siblina prefers me in green," Kamron muttered and wiped the back of his neck.

Lukas got in front of Kamron and grabbed either side of his tunic, giving him a little shake. "You need to get a hold of yourself."

Kamron shook his head and collapsed into a chair. "I just can't stop thinking this is one huge mistake."

"Okay, that's the exact opposite of what you should be thinking right now. What happened? You were in great spirits last night."

Kamron's face fell into his hands. Last night had been different. Easy. They were celebrating an end of an era in their friendship, and the start of a new future. They drank to love and reveled in memories. But now, as the clock clicked closer to noon, and Kamron prepared to step out into the great hall where friends, family, dignitaries, and other socialites waited for him, he couldn't do it. Not because he had stage fright or anything of the sort, but because he knew as soon as he stepped out there, he couldn't leave. And once he was out there, things would set into motion, and Siblina would join him, and then they would be married.

His stomach turned and he closed his lips tight.

"Come on, man, tell me where your head is at," Lukas pleaded, pulling a chair up across from him.

Kamron looked up at his best friend, silent for a long moment and then he let it out. "If the curse is going to target my heart's greatest wants and desires, then marrying Siblina is a mistake. I want her to be mine. If I end things here, then that's the curse fulfilled, and it can't hurt me anymore. If I marry her, and we build a life together, there are so many ways the curse could destroy it." He shook his head. "I can't risk her getting hurt because of me."

Lukas sighed and leaned back. "So ultimately you're wanting to ruin her life just to protect yourself from more harm."

"What?"

"You think cutting it off here will only hurt a little, when things potentially ending later will hurt more, so you want to end them now. To protect yourself. I get it."

"No, that's not it."

"How is it different?"

Kamron ran a hand over his face. "If I end things now, we both get hurt, but she lives. If we get married, we'll be happy, but maybe in a year, she dies in childbirth. My way, at least she lives."

Lukas shook his head. "Have you told her of your fears?"

"Of course. Everyone knows about the curse already, but I wanted to make sure she was prepared for the worst."

"And what did she say?"

Kamron stood up and paced back and forth in the small room he'd gotten ready in, trying to avoid the flowers and mirrors scattered throughout the room. Whose brilliant idea was it adding all the mirrors, anyway? No one needed this much self-reflection at a time like this. "She has that thing where she thinks she knows what's coming and what's best." He waved his hand through the air while he spoke. “She won’t tell me anything, because she doesn’t really know anything for sure, just feelings or hints of things.”

“But she thinks everything will work out?”

Kamron thought for a moment. He remembered the frown Siblina had gotten when they spoke about his fear of the curse. A little line in her forehead had formed, and she was quiet for a long time. “She said it doesn’t matter how things end. It only matters that we appreciate what we have while we have it, and that we work to make the world better for ourselves and for the future.”

“Sounds like something she’d say.”

“So I’m supposed to walk into this blind?”

“No. You’re supposed to walk into it with your eyes wide open and enjoy it, like she said.” Lukas picked up a gray cloth from the back of a chair. “Now shut up and let me tie your cravat before we’re late.”

The king and queen stood just inside the side door of the great hall, so Kamron ran into their alarmed faces when he opened the door.

“Everything going all right, boys?” Elodie asked.

“Yes, your Majesty. Kamron had trouble with his cuff links, but we got it sorted,” Lukas told her.

“Right.” Silas clapped his son on the shoulder. “You’re ready, then?”

Kamron took a deep breath. “As ready as I’ll ever be.”

“Excellent. Let’s get going then.” Elodie motioned for a footman while Silas led them to the front of the hall where a large arch, covered in trailing flowers from the queen’s personal garden, stood.

Nearing the front, a man stepped into their path. He had olive skin and gray eyes, with striped salt and pepper hair, though he looked about forty-five. From his chin hung a long pointy beard, very much out of fashion in the Twoshy.

“Gedas!” Kamron said, reaching for the man and pulling him

into a hug. “I didn’t think you would make it. It’s been so long since I’ve seen you.”

Gedas, or Wizard Gediminas, one of the most powerful mages in the world alongside Wizard Adelina. He had been his mother’s mentor through her life, and the only person who didn’t age and die over the century she spent popping in and out of this reality while under the spell of the Misplaced.

“Yes, well, you’ve been quite busy making a knight of yourself, and I was traveling,” the wizard said, a little stiffly, pulling out of his hug. He nodded a greeting to Lukas and Silas.

“Traveling? Have any fun adventures to share? My soon to be wife has been quite eager to meet you.” Kamron was babbling, but he didn’t know how to stop.

“I’ve been traveling here and there, but I might be able to scrape together a good tale after the wedding,” Gedas offered. “Oh, that reminds me.” He fumbled in his cloak and pulled out a wooden box the size of an apple and tossed it to Kamron, who caught it easily. It was a spell box, wrapped in layers of spells for Kamron to pick through and break in order to access the present inside. Kamron grinned. He loved unraveling magic, and Gedas’s puzzles were harder than most.

“Not traveling south, I hope,” Queen Elodie said, coming up beside the wizard.

“My Gull, how radiant you look,” Gedas said, using his nickname for her.

Elodie rolled her eyes. “I’m old and you are not. It’s quite unfair, you know.”

“Alas, you stayed younger than most for longer than most, but time vortices and a magical paradox have a way of catching up to a body.”

Kamron rolled his eyes at the old man. He looked forty, but no one knew how long he’d looked forty. Magic had a way of preserving life, and an abundance of magic, like the Elv had or a Hu wizard had, could extend life greatly. Although where an Elv aged slowly, a Hu wizard picked their age, aging or reversing its effects at will.

"What's wrong with traveling south?" Lukas asked.

"Nothing. Nothing at all is wrong with the south. Lots of great things to see," Gedas said.

"As long as you stay out of the mountains," Elodie said, looking pointedly at Gedas.

Kamron frowned at her. She was often disapproving and contradicting Gedas; they had a long history, but something else seemed to be going on as well.

"The mountains are not so bad, My Gull."

"The mountains are dangerous."

"Any place can be dangerous if you do not treat it with proper respect," Gedas added.

Yep. Definitely not talking about the mountains.

"Can we not bicker today?" Silas asked.

Elodie looked abashed and turned to Kamron. "We'll take our seats." She reached up and patted his cheek before letting Silas lead her away. Gedas nodded to Kamron and made his way to a seat. Lukas nudged Kamron, and they continued to the front.

Why would his mother be so worried about Gedas going to the mountains? The thought picked at the back of Kamron's brain like it was important. The Avi and Dwarv made the mountain home, but they were good people, they just didn't love living with the Hu. The only danger in the mountains was one of bedtime stories. An old wizard in a way Gedas was never old, who'd once used his magic to hurt the Twoshy. Gedas didn't see the wizard as a threat, and Elodie swore to never interfere, yet something needed to be done.

The ceremony started, with small children throwing petals in the air, and Kamron watched it all while thinking over threats to the south, but all that left his mind as the large doors at the end of the hall parted. His eyes fell on Siblina, who shimmered in silver and lavender, on her father's arm.

As she stepped closer, her eyes danced, and Kamron's heart slowed. Nothing else mattered in that moment, and he knew with absolute confidence that she was everything to him. His anxiety dissolved, as if it had never been, and the future stretched out before him and Siblina—theirs for the conquering.

When she reached him, he took her hands in his and swore he would never let go. They said their vows and were pronounced married, and he kissed his wife for all present, his mom wiping her tears in the front row.

The celebration that followed was one Kamron would never forget. He laughed and danced with his wife, and was congratulated for his lucky match by hundreds of people. After they ate, Siblina left for the bathroom, and Lukas slid into her seat. Kamron toasted his best friend.

"Feeling better, then?" Lukas asked.

Kamron shook his head. "Joy. Joy is the only thing I know now. Anything before this was insignificant nonsense."

Lukas laughed. "I'm glad. You and Siblina are a perfect match."

"But what about you? I can't be happy in my bliss until I know my best friend is as well," Kamron said, and Lukas sighed. "What?"

Lukas looked into the crowd of partygoers for a long moment.

"Do you think it's foolish to love someone who will outlive you so drastically?"

Kamron blew out a breath. "That's a hard one. If Siblina had more magic, enough to make her a wizard ranking and give her enough power to live forever, I would still marry her if she would have me."

Lukas grimaced. "My uncle told me I can't marry an Elv, because the children couldn't inherit. He said to keep her as a mistress and marry someone else."

"Your uncle said that?" Kamron was disgusted.

Lukas nodded. "He's not alone in his thinking."

"What about your parents?"

"They say it's my decision."

"It is. It's only your decision. Yours and the woman who agrees to it."

Siblina returned, and Kamron stood and pulled her into a hug. "I missed you, my love."

She giggled. "You can come next time if you wish."

Lukas groaned and stood up and left the table. "Married people are so weird."

Kamron and Siblina kissed again, to the cheers of all those around them, then they returned to their celebration. They danced, ate pastries, and danced some more. Kamron danced with his mom, and Siblina's mom, and her aunt, and her father, and then Siblina again. When they were laughing and out of breath, Kamron led Siblina out into the cool evening air of the garden, tiny light globes speckled about like starlight. They walked, enjoying the peace of the open air, and the lack of people congratulating them, happy to be alone for a moment.

"It won't work," Briony said on the other side of a topiary, and Kamron ducked behind it, pulling Siblina with him.

"Why not?" Lukas said. "Our people have married before. Look at your sister."

Siblina's mouth fell open, and Kamron grinned and nodded. They both stilled on the other side of the bush to listen.

"Yes, but my sister's husband isn't responsible for producing an heir to a Hu kingdom."

"But that doesn't matter."

"Yes, it does. Rohap will never allow a half Elv with a centuries long life take over their nation. You'll be pressured to produce a crownable heir, and I'd castrate you before I tolerate you taking another wife or mistress."

Siblina's eyes got big and Kamron clamped his lips together to keep from laughing. Siblina shook her head at him and covered his mouth with her soft hands.

"That's romantic of you," Lukas said, and Kamron could hear the smile in his voice. "I'd let you castrate me if I ever strayed. But

I won't. I love you, Briony. And I don't care about producing an heir. No. No, hear me. I care about children. I want to have a load of children and then I want to force one of them to marry one of Siblina and Kamron's kids so that we can all be in-laws."

Siblina's eyebrows went up, and she glared at Kamron. Kamron nodded and grinned into her hand. He and Lukas had planned the whole thing the night before. They'd each have a lot of kids so they had more options, and hopefully two of them went to the altar willingly.

"I care about children, but not about heirs," Lukas continued. "I have enough brothers and sisters. They can produce the heirs to take over when I die. All I want is for you to be by my side before then."

They went silent, and Kamron grimaced, sure they were kissing. Siblina, however grinned, and he rolled his eyes at her. She didn't take the hint, so he licked her palm, still covering his mouth. She gasped and pulled her hand away, then they both froze, afraid of being found out. But they didn't hear anything. Siblina wiped her hand on his chest and mouthed, "That's gross."

Kamron smiled and leaned down, and Siblina tipped her head back for a kiss. He licked her nose instead. She made a face and pushed him, but he held her tight. They were married now, and she was his to lick as he pleased.

"Is that a yes, then?" Lukas asked, and Briony was quiet for a long moment.

"If I said no, would you leave me alone?"

"Nope. I would abdicate my position and follow you around like a little lost puppy for the rest of my life."

More silence followed until Briony sighed. "Fine! I'll marry you. But only if you promise not to spend the whole time complaining about your age."

"I promise, my love."

"I don't care if you get gray hair and wrinkles," Briony said, continuing her rant. "Aging is beautiful and natural and if I have to hear you complain about it, I'll make you suffer as much as I do."

"Of course, my love. I'll cherish every gray."

"You're impossible."

Lukas laughed. "Yes, but you love me. Even if you won't say it."

"Because this is a bad idea, and I didn't want to encourage you."

"I think I'm a bit past encouraged at this point."

"Yes, I know. And I'm too much in love with you for my sensibilities to make any wise decisions."

"Briony, don't cry. Please, what's wrong?"

"It's just that I know I'll have to see you die and then somehow I'll have to keep going. I'll have to go on living without you."

Kamron reached out and wiped a tear off Siblina's cheek.

"Truthfully, it's better this way. You're so much stronger than I am, and I don't think I could bear losing you," Lukas said.

Siblina and Kamron quietly stepped away from the topiary, leaving the garden and returning to the party, knowing they wouldn't be heard over the sounds of their friend's tears.

# Chapter Twelve

"Gonna get me sacked, he is," Bruno muttered under his breath but still loud enough for Kamron to hear him as he grabbed the tea tray.

"Bruno, you're not going to get fired. I pay your salary."

"You might be paying my salary, but we both know it's your misses who makes the final decisions."

"I promise this isn't a trick or a prank, okay? Just wait till Lady Siblina gets dressed, then run me down the corresponding tunic. She's sleeping in and I need to get to work."

Bruno grumbled a little more, but he didn't disagree, which was as much of an acceptance as Kamron would get. He thanked the man and descended the stairs to his office.

Married life agreed with him. Kamron loved waking up next to his wife every morning and falling asleep next to her every night. They ate breakfast together, took long walks in the mornings, enjoyed lunch, and relaxed in the afternoons before dinner. The only time he dragged himself away for work was when she had work of her own, setting up her charity school to train young mages who didn't have enough power for a scholarship to the university. She taught practical working magic, perfect for building a life for oneself.

After six months of marriage, Kamron was behind at work. He pored over maps and field reports looking for patterns in the recent border attacks, but it all held the same. It didn't make sense for Vasniydor to keep up these border raids for years. If it was just a distraction, they should have done something else by now.

A little before lunchtime, there was a knock on Kamron's door.

"Enter."

Bruno carried a folded lilac tunic. Kamron stood and squeezed around his small desk, taking the shirt from his favorite servant.

"Ah, she went with the lilac today. Thank you, Bruno."

Bruno nodded. "Her maid also said the lady planned to stop by the healer."

"Good." Kamron pulled off his gray tunic and handed it over to Bruno, who folded it while he put on the new one. "She hasn't been sleeping well."

"The palace healers should have her right as rain in no time," Bruno said, before excusing himself from the office.

Kamron let out a sigh. He hoped so. He didn't like anything being off with her. Every night for the last two weeks, nightmares interrupted her sleep, and while Kamron held her as she sobbed or retched over the images her mind produced, he felt helpless.

Kamron went back to his desk and pulled three rolled maps from a shelf above. Unfurling them, his eyes fell over a part of the country that was not being raided by the enemy but weighed heavier in his mind. He ran a finger over the inked lines suggesting the rise and fall of mountains, ending with a cliff face in the shape of an outstretched bat wing. This was his newest map, and his prized possession. He'd spent the last few months collecting maps of southern Aluna and the Tokke Mountains, trying to find anything that referenced the stories and tales his mother had once told him of her trip to the cave where Wizard Viclor lived.

His mother's one warning his entire life was to leave the wizard alone. Don't enter the mountains and disturb him, don't do anything to upset the peace they now had. Because of that, his mother never explained where in the mountains to find the wizard, other than a cave at the base of a cliff that looked like the outstretched wing of a bat. This map was the only Kamron had ever found with a suggested location of such a mountain. It wasn't exactly clear directions, but it was a start.

His door opened, and Siblina entered, wearing a lilac morning dress. She was beautiful and elegant, if not a little tired. Kamron stood and squeezed around his desk, pulling her in for a hug. "How are you feeling?"

"Fine," she said with a small yawn. "We're matching."

"I know." Kamron kissed her forehead. "It's a wonder how that keeps happening. As if marriage has made us so in sync."

Siblina looked up and narrowed her eyes at him. "Sure it has."

He kissed her nose. "So, what did the healer say?"

Siblina sighed and snuggled into his chest. "There are no secrets in this castle."

"True enough. So spill. Are they able to give you a sleeping draft of some sort?"

"No, that would be bad for the baby."

Kamron froze. It took his mind longer than his body to understand what his wife had said, and when he did, his heart pounded in his ears, and he desperately needed a drink of water.

Siblina looked up at him, but he wasn't sure at first what to say.

"We're going to have a baby," Siblina said.

Kamron closed his mouth with a clack and ran a hand down his face. "Are you sure?"

"Yes."

A small grin crept onto his face. A baby. He knew it would happen eventually, and it had always been a part of the plan, but he couldn't quite believe eventually was now. He laughed and picked Siblina up, spinning her around. She laughed and smiled along with him.

"How long?"

"It's only been a few weeks."

Kamron frowned. "You've only been having bad dreams a few weeks."

"And hopefully they won't last for all nine months." Siblina yawned again, and her jaw cracked.

"Will you tell me what you're dreaming? Maybe talking about it will make it better."

She shook her head and pressed her face against his chest. "It won't."

"Whatever it is, you don't need to carry it on your own."

"I do. It's my burden to bear."

Something cold ran down Kamron's back. "So, the dreams are of the future?" He'd suspected as much but didn't want to press.

She pulled away but not out of his arms. "It's not as clear as you might think. Mostly they are emotions or hints of a picture nudging me in one direction or another. I know something is coming, but I couldn't tell you what. I only know my magic will guide me in the right direction when it gets here." She turned further into his grasp and ran a hand over the parchment on his desk. "Is this the Tokke Mountains?"

"Yes. I'm keeping an eye on all our borders."

"What's this symbol here?" she asked.

"That's for a small village too insignificant to name." Kamron looked and saw she pointed to a small point near the southwest coast of Aluna. A tiny speck of a village with the Variant Forest surrounding it from the north and west, and the Tokke Mountains to the south. Only a small road sandwiched between the forest and mountains allowed travelers to reach it. Kamron pulled out a more detailed map of the spot and spread it on the table. "Here, see how isolated it is? We send people with each census, and merchants sometimes go there to trade because the Avi do, but other than that it's totally isolated."

"What's it called?"

"Ascella. It means armpit because it's in the crook of the Variant Forest."

Siblina snorted but didn't take her eyes off the map, trailing the path with her finger. "Really?"

Kamron nodded. "Remind me to tell you stories of that forest. Gedas took me as a boy and there's some fun folklore about a magical beast who eats travelers."

"That sounds delightful. I'm so glad you had such positive influences as a child."

"Don't worry, I'm sure Gedas will be happy to take our child camping and tell him the same tales."

Siblina turned from the map at last and smiled carefully at her husband. "Are you happy?"

Kamron leaned down and kissed her gently.

"Happier than I could ever believe possible. Can we tell Lukas when we see them this weekend?"

Siblina rolled her eyes.

Since their wedding two months ago, Briony and Lukas had been in a little bubble of newlywed happiness, and the two couples hadn't seen each other. Lukas orb called Kamron the night before to see if he and Siblina wanted to visit for the weekend and catch up.

"I forgot we were going."

"We can cancel, if you want."

"No, I miss them too. We can tell them about the baby, but keep in mind it's still really early. We don't want word to go too far."

Kamron picked the orb off his desk and tossed it in the air, catching it easily. "So, should we orb your parents, then go crash lunch with mine?" he asked, smiling.

Siblina took the orb from his hand and leaned against him. "That sounds like an excellent idea. Your dad will cry, and your mom will offer me something for my tea or bath to help with the pregnancy."

Kamron laughed and kissed her forehead. He was beyond

happy at their news, but still a little voice in the back of his mind warned him time ran short to protect his future. He needed to act.

They set off the next morning for Arnav, taking a little longer than planned to rise and get on the road. Siblina insisted on riding, though Kamron tried to coax her into a carriage. As they ascended the palace road, Kamron spotted a familiar figure sitting on the steps to the palace.

Lukas stood as they brought their horses to a stop. "Took you long enough," he said, as a stable hand came for their horses. Lukas pulled out an orb and squeezed it before talking into it. "Briony, they're here."

"You're such a dork," Briony replied through the orb.

"Love you too," Lukas said, squeezing the orb off and dropping it in his pocket.

Kamron helped Siblina from her horse, then embraced his friend. "We got a late start this morning."

"I get it." Lukas guided his friends up the steps and into the castle. "I'm just not as important as I used to be in your life."

"Oh good. I'm glad you understand and I don't have to explain it to you." Kamron punched Lukas hard in the side, but he dodged the bulk of it. He returned the punch with one aimed at Kamron's chest, but it didn't connect as he spun out of the way.

"So glad things never change," Briony said, coming down the hall.

Kamron broke away from the scuffle and they said their polite hellos. He wanted to burst out his happy news now that they were all together again, but he wasn't sure it was the right time. He and Siblina should have talked about it. Maybe she would want to be the one to say it.

Kamron pondered his options while Lukas led them up to their sitting room where tea and lunch was spread out. His foot tapped a rhythm against the carpet while he poured his wife tea and waited for an opening.

“There’s something we wanted to tell you,” Lukas said, looking at his wife.

Kamron couldn’t wait any longer. “We’re pregnant!” he burst out.

“We are!” Lukas said equally ecstatic, and the two men hugged. “Wait. How did you know?”

Kamron pulled away from Lukas, confused at the question. “The healer told Siblina yesterday.”

“Well, that’s quite a breach of confidentiality, isn’t it? You aren’t playing one of your tricks and spying, are you?”

“What? No. This isn’t a joke. We’re really pregnant.”

“I know we are, but—”

Briony put her hand over her husband’s mouth and pulled him back, while Siblina stepped in front of Kamron.

“You two really are dense,” Briony said.

Siblina laughed and turned to the other woman. They hugged and laughed. “How far along are you?” she asked.

“About a month and a half. You?”

“Maybe a few weeks. Not far.”

Kamron blinked. He looked at Briony, then at Lukas. “You’re pregnant?”

Lukas nodded. “You too?”

Kamron nodded.

“Technically, neither of you are pregnant. We are you, loobies,” Briony said, but her words were meaningless.

Kamron and Lukas broke out into big smiles and embraced again, before high-fiving. “Operation marry the kids is a go,” Lukas said.

Kamron laughed. “Another twenty years or so and we’ll be brothers-in-law.”

“That’s not how that works either,” Siblina said.

But the two princes didn’t care. Instead, they chatted about everything they would do with their children, forgetting their wives completely.

They had a wonderful weekend reconnecting and celebrating their new partners, and the future life soon entering their families. Siblina's nightmares didn't end because they were visiting friends, and it was as if the nightly episodes were her own sort of morning sickness, brought on by the pregnancy.

She woke queasy and uncomfortable on their last morning in Rohap. It didn't sit well with Kamron, Siblina's potentially prophetic nightmares warning of some danger, just as their baby came into existence. Their child would be the greatest weakness in Kamron's world. Wizard Viclor targeted the babies and heirs of all the rulers in Kamron's grandfather's age. What was to keep him from targeting Kamron's new baby?

He paced back and forth in their bedroom while Siblina cleaned up in the bathroom. He had to protect Siblina and the baby at all costs.

"What's wrong?" Siblina asked, coming back into the room, a little pale.

Kamron moved to her side and pulled her into a hug. "I think I need to make a trip, but the timing couldn't be worse. I don't want to leave you."

"Where are you going?"

"There's a threat that we need to protect Aluna from." Kamron stroked her head, not sure how much to tell her. "I need to ask one of my commanders if he's willing to volunteer for the mission. It's dangerous, and I think it's best if I ask him in person."

Siblina sighed and pulled away from him and searched through her wardrobe. "How long do you expect to be gone?"

"That's it?"

"What do you mean?"

"We're newlyweds and you're pregnant. You aren't upset I'm even considering a journey?"

Siblina smiled and pulled out a pink dress. "For all the reasons you just said, I know you wouldn't consider it if it wasn't important."

"Right. Well if I rush, I might be six weeks." Kamron pulled a matching pink tunic out of his bag and pulled it over his head.

"We can handle six weeks apart." Siblina traded the pink dress for a green frock and trousers. "Pregnancies are long and boring. You won't miss anything special."

Kamron pulled off his pink tunic and dug through his bag until he found the green one. "Every moment with you is special. Promise you'll tell Mum about your dreams. Maybe she can think of something that will help that won't hurt the baby." He grinned when he said the word baby and put on the green tunic.

At breakfast, Kamron noticed how much thinner Briony was. He hadn't noticed, so concerned as he was with Siblina. Briony was only a few weeks ahead of Siblina in her pregnancy, and he worried if his wife would be okay while he was gone. He'd have to have his mother keep an eye on her.

It took him a day short of three weeks to make the journey to the border with Vasniydor. Kamron took two horses to trade off often and keep a heavy pace. He settled into an inn a short ride from the camp where his favorite commander was stationed and wandered into the camp assessing how things were going. He spoke to a range of soldiers to get a better picture of events. Kamron knew someone had spread news of his presence when he spotted Commander Rightwitch crossing a training field toward him.

"Sir Kamron. Congratulations on your recent nuptials," the older commander said.

"Thank you. Good to see you, Rightwitch."

"You as well. Though I must say, I'm surprised. I didn't expect to see you out this way at least till your second anniversary."

Kamron grinned. "Truthfully, I would have waited till the fifth, but matters forced my hand."

"Oh?"

"Perhaps we can chat in your office."

Rightwitch nodded and led the way through the camp to a

large command tent with maps and diagrams on the walls and a large table filled with a model of the terrain. He dismissed a few clerks and tapped a silencing charm on the wall of the tent. Kamron felt the spells of a standard charm flair around them. Their conversation would be private.

Rightwitch gestured to a chair while he grabbed a tea kettle and two mugs off a side table.

Kamron settled into the chair. “Have you enjoyed your time at the border?”

Rightwitch filled a mug and pushed it to Kamron. “Sure enough. I’m a simple man who enjoys following orders.”

Kamron almost snorted. Rightwitch was one of the sharpest people he knew. They had worked closely through the previous years and he trusted the man’s advice and intuition. “How would you feel about a change of scenery?”

“Well, I’ve never been much of one for city life, but what did you have in mind?”

Kamron looked into his tea and gave it a sniff. “How about the mountains? I’ve heard the thin air does wonders for the complexion.”

“And what would we be doing in the mountains?” Rightwitch asked, his expression growing curious.

“Bird watching,” Kamron told him. He would think Kamron meant the Avi people. Like the Elv, Hu, and Dwarv, Avi was another race of men, this one with feathers in place of hair and talons in place of feet. They were a secluded people, happy to keep away from the Hu high in the mountains.

“Bird watching? What kind of birds?”

“The work and the specifics will be classified. I need your decision and vow before telling you more. It will be potentially dangerous, but I’m hoping it doesn’t go beyond boring surveillance work. The threat I send you to look out for could be one of the greatest Aluna has faced, and while it might not be as urgent as the threat here at the border, it could be deadlier. I would ask for you to pick a handful of your favorite soldiers, volunteer only. I don't know how long I will need you to stay in the mountains. The team could rotate out, but I would like to keep as little activity as possible so not to raise suspicions."

Rightwitch nodded, taking it all in as he sipped his tea. "When would we depart?"

"I would like to see you go before the frost sets in and the weather makes your trip impossible. I have a rough idea of the location, but it will take a little wayfinding. You'll need to build a base and dig in, somewhere close to the target but where you can withstand the winter without being observed."

"I'm in." Rightwitch set down his tea. "Give me the details."

Kamron pulled a map out of his tunic and told the commander about the cave in the mountains, and the wizard living within.

He spent three days briefing Rightwitch on the threat and assessing his team. There were eight in total, and Kamron knew them all. They were capable and competent. When things were settled and the team turned their focus to supplies and packing, Kamron packed his own bag. He carried his bag out to the stables when he spotted a familiar horse. Grinning, he wandered into the dining room of the inn and looked about. Sure enough, a man in his forties or so, with a long pointy beard, sat at a table paying homage to a thick slice of meatloaf.

"Gedas," Kamron said, and sat across from the old wizard.

Gedas looked up and frowned at him. "Shouldn't you be on the other side of the country with your wife?"

Kamron laughed. "Yes, actually. I'm leaving now. I had business at the border."

Gedas nodded. "I'm glad you aren't so absorbed in matrimony that you're slacking on your duties."

Kamron bit his lip. That might have been exactly what he'd been doing for the last few months. "What brings you here?"

"Just a spot of lunch. Kammy makes the best meatloaf," Gedas said, not answering the question. “Wait for me and I’ll go with you east.”

Kamron nodded and settled into his chair. He would feel better having Gedas in Tate where he could keep Siblina that much safer, but the wizard would slow him down on the journey.

Once Gedas finished his lunch and graciously accepted a second portion wrapped in beeswax cloth for later, they set off for home.

The journey took longer. When they reached three weeks on the road and were not yet home, Kamron’s worry for Siblina grew too strong. He asked Lukas to check on her, confident his mother would downplay any issues. The next day after lunch, his orb glowed, and he answered it, relieved to see Lukas’s face. “How are you?” Kamron asked.

“Good. I’m leaving Tate now.”

“How’s Siblina?”

“She’s well but says to stop worrying. She’s not sleeping well, but she says the morning sickness has passed. And she looks great.”

“Truly?”

“Yes, she’s glowing,” Lukas said, but he didn’t seem pleased. It was hard to tell in the rounded picture of the orb, but his eyes looked worried.

“What’s wrong?”

“It’s not Siblina, it’s Briony.”

“What is it?” Kamron asked.

“She’s had terrible morning sickness the entire pregnancy. We thought that’s all it was, and the healers agreed, but it’s gotten worse. Seeing Siblina, it hit me just how much weight Briony’s lost.”

“Have my mum stop in. She’ll do it. You know she will, and she’ll be mad if she finds out you didn’t ask.”

Lukas smiled a little. “Okay, I will. When will you be back?”

“About a week.”

"All right. I'll see you then."

"Everything all right?" Gedas said, riding up closer to Kamron.

"Yes. I don't know why I'm worried. I'm sure it's nothing."

The wizard tapped his chin, as he often did when he wanted to sound important. "Children have a way of distressing their caretakers in ways unimaginable."

Kamron grinned. "Did Mum distress you often?"

"She did, although I believe you paid her back tenfold."

"Would you mind checking in on my friend's wife once you've settled in?"

"I'm not a nursemaid," Gedas said grumpily.

"No, but she is sarcastic, which I know you appreciate, and she's Elv, so it would be diplomatic of you."

"Well I suppose, if she's sarcastic, then I must help."

Kamron grinned and urged his horse to go faster.

# Chapter Thirteen

"Run me a bath, would you?" Siblina asked, and Kamron held in a groan. He was utterly exhausted, but he knew for every yawn and crick in his neck, his wife felt it tenfold.

Kamron nodded and bypassed his bed toward the bathroom. He poured some of his mother's healing herb mix into a little bag and turned on the faucet. His wife liked a hot bath, and he waited till it steamed before plugging up the tub and dropping in the herb bag. Just like a giant mug of tea. He grinned. He really was tired.

Having a newborn was wonderful. Terrifying and exhausting, and absolutely wonderful. Their son, Keth, was born on a cool fall night under a crescent moon. He was healthy and beautiful, and Kamron couldn't be prouder.

He left the bathroom and crossed to the bed where his wife nursed the baby. He kissed her and ran a finger over Keth's cheek.

"Have you heard from Lukas?" Siblina asked, a hint of worry in the line on her forehead.

Kamron shook his head. Briony had been unwell through her pregnancy, and her labor two weeks before was hard. Her sister came to care for her in the last few months of her pregnancy and was so worried she sent for an Elv healer. The baby, Gabriel, was healthy, but Briony faded.

The orb on his bedside table glowed. He sighed and picked it up, hopeful it wasn't anything that required putting on boots. Lukas's face appeared in the glass, gaunt and frightened. "What's wrong?"

"I need you. When can you get here?" Lukas asked.

"I'm putting on my boots now."

"Thank you."

Kamron set down the orb and turned to Siblina, quietly shushing the baby. "I'm sorry, love."

But Siblina shook her head. "We're fine. Go and orb me when you find out what's happening."

He kissed her and Keth, and pulled on his boots. "I'm sending in a nursemaid to take him for the night. You need your sleep and I won't be here to help."

Siblina sighed. "I really didn't want to be one of those wives who never touches their children."

Kamron laughed. "I know, and you aren't. But you need a break."

Siblina nodded. He kissed her again and called a maid before leaving.

He rode through the night and when he reached the castle in Arnav, dead on his feet, a footman led him into Briony and Lukas's room. The air was heavy with tension, and when Lukas noticed him, he rose from his chair next to Briony's side of the bed and crossed to Kamron, gripping his arm hard. Lukas looked horrible, like he hadn't slept in days. Kamron braced himself.

"She's dying."

Kamron shook his head. "But she's Elv."

"That's the problem. It's some disease that only affects the Elv. They call it the Slayer," Lukas said, with something angry and wild in his eyes.

"What does Gedas say?" He'd been staying at the castle for the last few weeks when Briony grew worse.

Lukas's grip on his arm tightened, and he shook Kamron a little. "He doesn't know anything about it. That's why all the healers we called were useless."

"But they have to have a cure. The Elv have such long lives," Kamron reasoned.

But as Lukas's eyes grew more and more bleak, he knew the answer. Lukas dropped his head and Kamron pulled him close, letting him sob into his tunic. When at last he could speak, Lukas's voice was bitter. "It was supposed to be me. I was supposed to die first. This is all wrong."

"Sorry to upset your plan, Your Highness," Briony croaked out, and in a moment Lukas was at her side, helping her drink water through a straw.

"How are you feeling, my love?"

But Briony didn't look at him, focusing her attention on Kamron. "Don't let him mourn me too long. He has enough life left. He can live and love again." Her voice broke, and she drank more. "I can't tell him, because he won't listen—"

"You're right, I won't."

"—so you have to remind him. Okay?"

Kamron nodded. He didn't think he could speak, but he nodded in the hopes it conveyed his heart without letting the pain in his chest burst out.

Briony held his gaze for a moment longer and then sunk back into her pillows. "I told you not to fall in love with me."

"Shush," Lukas told her. "You know that was never a possibility."

The door opened and Kamron saw Kody, Briony's sister, stick her head inside and gesture for him. He excused himself and joined her in Lukas's sitting room. Kody was much taller than her half sister, with green swirls winding over her brown skin despite being only half Elv, her mother had been Hu. Just as Gabe would be half Elv and half Hu, and just like Kody, he would never know his mother.

"Is he right? Is there no chance?" he asked.

Kody ran a hand down her face, showing similar exhaustion as Lukas, but where Lukas was desperate, Kody was angry.

"The Elv think they are invulnerable. It's why this sickness is such a killer. It can only be defeated in its early stages, and by the time it's identified, it's too late."

"Is there anything that can be done?"

"There are always things we can try, but none of them have ever helped anyone else."

Kamron shook his head. "But we can still try. I'll send my mum, and I know a good healer in Tross."

"You need to take the baby," Kody said.

"What?"

"It's contagious. In the late stages, a rash forms and any with Elv blood can catch it if the right precautions aren't taken."

Kamron shook his head. "We can't take Briony's baby when she doesn't have much time left. Can't you just keep him protected?"

Kody sighed and leaned back in her chair. "Do you really think Briony could handle seeing her baby in the same room as her and not be able to touch him? Wouldn't that be worse torture than her knowing he's safe with dear friends who will care for him as if he were their own?"

"I need to orb my wife."

"You also need to take a nap. You're traveling home with a two-week-old baby."

Siblina cried when Kamron told her about Briony. They worried over her for weeks, but the finality of the knowledge was the worst. They had magic. Death from sickness shouldn't be an option, and when it was, it became a tragedy.

He didn't sleep, but he did nap fitfully until he was confident he could ride his horse without falling off. He said goodbye to Briony and Lukas, and cried as they said goodbye to their son.

Baby Gabe didn't cry. He was a happy sort of baby, all gassy smiles. Kamron rode his horse and followed the carriage carrying Gabe and his nursemaid who would come with him to Tate. An hour from home, Kamron's pocket glowed, and a small spark of dread shot down his spine, but it was only a routine report from the border. There was another raid attack, but nothing out of the ordinary. As he sighed off and made to put the orb back in his pocket, it glowed again. This time, Commander Rightwitch's face looked back at him. Kamron slowed his horse so he wouldn't be overheard.

"Rightwitch, how goes it?"

A month earlier, Rightwitch's team found the cave shaped like a wing, after a long search, and set up camp on a ridge above. There was one clear entrance to the cave, and from Queen Elodie's story, Kamron knew at least one other entrance existed. After a month of watching, they had seen the wizard only once when he came out of his cave to lay on the hard stone and stare up at the sky for three hours in the late morning, before returning to his cave, and not reemerging.

"Rian hasn't checked in for over thirty hours," Rightwitch said.

"What?" Kamron's pulse rose. What else could go wrong in the world?

"He was on the watch detail. They check in every three hours. He skipped his time. I've sent a few others out looking for him three times and they can't find a trace of him."

"Any idea where he would have gone? Did he have a lover or a tendency to drink?"

"No." It was a hard no. Kamron knew Rian, and knew he didn't have any vices, but it was worth asking.

"What trouble could someone get to in the mountains? There aren't any predators."

"None that we've seen so far," Rightwitch said.

"Right. Anything else?"

"No."

"Keep me informed."

Kamron signed off and shoved the orb back in his pocket, his blood pressure pulsing through a vein in his neck. His responsibilities felt like too much to juggle, and he wasn't even king yet. His parents made it look so effortless; he didn't know if he was cut out for leadership.

He urged his horse into a trot to catch up with the carriage. He needed to get home.

Life with two babies almost seemed easier than life with one. Siblina couldn't do it all herself, so she didn't try. Iris, Kamron's second cousin, was the biggest help of all. Tross was her home, and she knew the castle well, helping with general household management, but now she was always there to lend an extra set of hands or scoop up a crying baby.

Gabe's first birthday arrived, and Lukas canceled, not wanting to leave Briony as her illness worsened. It would be a small affair, held in the king and queen's personal garden. Kamron and Iris hung a banner with Siblina to correct the height.

"A little higher on the right," she called.

The door to the garden opened slowly, and Bruno stuck his head in.

"Just a moment, Bruno," Kamron said as he lifted his corner. "Come on, woman. Both sides can't possibly need to go higher to make it level." Kamron complained.

"Well, I suppose that will have to do," Siblina said.

Kamron stuck the sticking spell for the banner as Iris fixed her side, and then he relaxed onto his heels. "Okay, Bruno, what did you need?"

Bruno looked put out and glanced at the ladies in the room before muttering. "Prince Lukas is in the nursery."

"He is?" Kamron asked, delighted by the news. "I didn't think he was coming."

Bruno shook his head. "He's a bit distraught, and the nurse didn't know what to do."

Kamron frowned and motioned for his wife to stay before heading up to the nursery.

Two nursemaids and a footman stood in the hall outside of the room as Kamron approached. Growing more alarmed by the moment, he ducked into the nursery where both boys should have been napping before the celebration. He was greeted by the deep sobs of a man in pain. Lukas sat on the floor in a heap, a small bundle in his arms as he rocked back and forth, crying.

Kamron knelt beside his friend and put his hand on his shoulder. He already knew in his gut, and he didn't want to ask.

"She's gone," Lukas choked out, before collapsing into sobs again, and holding his son close to his chest.

Gabe wasn't crying but had tears in his little eyes as he rested his little palm on his father's face. Kamron cried and held his friend. He couldn't imagine his friend's sorrow, and the realities of Briony's death terrified Kamron.

Lukas stayed for two nights and left quietly the following morning. He asked Kamron and Siblina to keep Gabe for a time longer so he could deal with his loss without pushing his emotions onto his son.

Kamron took Gabe and Keth to his parents' private garden for lunch, and let them crawl around in the clover field. Neither baby walked yet, but they were close, and it became a bit of a betting pool to see which baby prince would be first. Elodie and Silas spent the afternoon standing each baby up and trying to coax them into walking, until the babies passed out from exhaustion, and the grandparents were ready to do the same. Kamron carried Keth inside, while Elodie carried Gabe.

"Oh, Mum, do you have that lotion for Keth's diaper rash you told me about?" Kamron asked.

"Let me get it." Elodie lay the sleeping baby on a couch in the sitting room as she ducked into the bathroom, and Kamron set Keth next to Gabe. Silas stretched out on a long lounge chair, looking just as ready for a nap as the babies.

Elodie returned to the room as a commotion broke out in the hallway outside of their rooms. Silas was up in an instant, and Kamron blinked. Where did he grab a sword from? His father never ceased to impress him. Silas moved to the door and opened it a crack. "What's happening?"

"Your Majesty, we can't stop him," a guard said. Kamron moved until he could see around his father. A soldier in a dirty and torn Alunan uniform fought against two guards that attempted to restrain him.

"What is the meaning of this, soldier?" Silas asked. But the man didn't respond. Elodie came up behind Kamron, and the soldier turned toward her. Kamron inhaled sharply. "What?" Silas asked.

"That's Rian. He's under Commander Rightwitch." He bit his lip. Kamron stepped forward and approached the man. "Rian, can you hear me?" His eyes were wide and slightly crazed as he fought against the guards. "Let him go," Kamron ordered.

The guards hesitated before releasing him. Rian straightened, then turned toward the queen. Then his demeanor changed. He bowed and started dancing, his eyes vacant and empty as he twirled around the hall, as if leading an invisible partner.

"Shall I call for the head sorcerer, Your Majesty?" a guard asked.

"Is Gedas still here?" Silas asked.

"Yes."

"Ask him to come instead."

The guard left and Rian danced for the next twenty-five minutes, sweat dripping down his dirty face. They tried to get his attention, offer him food or water, but he didn't respond to any of them. Kamron tried to feel for the magic controlling the man. He could sense it but couldn't reach inside of him and unravel it like he could a puzzle box.

Gedas entered the hallway with a chuckle. "Good to know you've grown so demanding of entertainment in your old age, Your Majesties, but I don't believe I could put on such a good show."

"Gedas, look closer," Elodie said.

Gedas frowned and stepped closer to Rian. His frown deepened with curiosity. He stepped closer still and grabbed Rian's arm as he passed, but Rian shook him off.

"Can he be made to stop?" Gedas asked.

"We haven't tried."

"Do it," he said to the guards, and Silas nodded in agreement.

Two of the guards stepped forward and waited for Rian to pass close and grabbed him. He put up a fight, resisting, and a third guard jumped in, trying to pin him to the ground. Rian threw a punch, connecting with a guard, while the other two wrestled him down. Rian fought them, resisting until his arm snapped. Kamron could feel the break in his chest.

"Release him," Silas ordered. The guards did, and Rian picked himself up, not using his right arm, and continued dancing, the broken arm hanging at an unnatural angle while he moved around the hall. He breathed heavily, and a few tears ran down his red, pain-stricken face, but still he danced.

"Gedas, do you know what this is?" Elodie asked.

"I believe I do. I believe I can counter the effects, but it will take time to brew."

Elodie stepped forward. "Will you teach me?"

"Of course, My Gull."

Elodie followed Gedas out.

Silas crossed to Kamron and spoke softly. "This man was under Commander Rightwitch?"

"Yes, I believe so. Rightwitch reported him missing several months ago."

"Missing from where?"

Kamron's heart picked up. He didn't want his father to know he'd done the one thing his mother warned him not to do. "They were deployed to the southern border, investigating complaints of robbers on the southern trading routes."

Silas's look darkened. "Did they go into the mountains?"

"No, why would they?" Kamron lied. "The bandits are reported to be Hu not Avi."

Silas relaxed. "Order Rightwitch and his team north."

"Sir, he reported two days ago they have a lead on the bandits. It's a large band that's been terrorizing merchants and the small villages."

"All right. Tell him to stay clear of the mountains at any cost. If the bandits are in the foothills, lure them out but don't send anyone in, understood?"

"Yes, sir."

Silas nodded. "Keep me informed of the situation."

Silas turned back to the dancing Rian, watching him closely.

It took Gedas six hours to create his counter potion. Kamron and Silas took turns watching Rian with the guards and watching the boys. Deciding not to risk walking them past the mindless man.

The guards wrestled Rian to the ground in order to get him to drink the concoction Gedas made, but Rian was a good fighter. A lot of the potion spilled until a soldier with a black eye came up with the idea to dance with Rian. She matched his steps, slowly taking lead and when she dipped Rian, the queen managed to pour the thick black slime into his mouth.

It took less than a minute for the effects to appear. First Rian's face seemed to sink, then his feet stopped moving. A moment later, he collapsed into a curled-up weeping mess on the floor. He passed out when the awaiting healers swooped in to set his arm. Once they carried him out of the hall, off to the healer's rooms, Silas turned to Elodie and Gedas. "We need to talk."

"Shall I join father?" Kamron asked.

"No, please get in contact with Rightwitch."

"Of course," Kamron agreed, but he did not.

Kamron carried the boys back to his sitting room, where a worried Siblina waited for him. She'd heard the short version of what happened, but grilled Kamron for the details while she kissed Gabe's neck rolls and got him to laugh.

Iris entered the room without knocking.

"Where's Lukas?" she asked.

"Back in Arnav by now," Kamron told her.

"What? Why? Gabe is still here."

"We're going to keep him a while longer, aren't we?" Siblina said to Gabe in a baby voice.

"Why wouldn't he take his son back?" Iris said.

"He doesn't want his son exposed to his grief."

Iris glared at Kamron, her expression angrier than he'd ever seen on her face, even as kids when he and Lukas had excluded her from their games.

"How can you just abandon your friend at a time like this?" she asked.

"He asked to be alone."

"And you're foolish enough to think that's what he actually needs?" She shook her head and left the room.

He looked to Siblina. "What's her problem?"

Siblina rolled her eyes. "She's probably about to pack for Arnav."

"Why?"

She shot a look at Kamron that said he was being stupid.

"He said he wanted time alone," Kamron said defensively.

"Yes, but Iris won't count."

"How do you know?"

"It's a woman thing."

Kamron rolled his eyes and tickled Keth. He had more important things to figure out than the chaos of his cousin's mind. The death of Briony drove home the realities. His life was on the edge of unraveling. Everything he'd ever wanted or wished for his future was only a ticking clock away from ruin. Lukas's wife died from a wasting disease and Lukas didn't even have a family curse. What was to prevent the same or some other threat from reaching Siblina or the boys? He had to shore up their defenses. He couldn't think about anything else.

The next morning, Kamron checked on Rian. He had no memory of the last few months, but the trauma of the events seemed to linger in his mind. He was twitchy and paranoid. Kamron left the healers' rooms, debating if he should tell Rightwitch when he next checked in. He decided he would if anything else happened, but for now, observing Wizard Viclor's actions were the most important thing.

# Chapter Fourteen

Around the castle of Tate, there was only one truth. A toddler prince always got his way.

Keth and Gabe were two of the happiest and most spoiled babies in the Twoshy. They weren't dissimilar in appearance, both having mixed colors between their parents, and with Gabe's green swirls not yet showing, only the slight point to his ears gave away his mixed heritage. Kody, who visited often, said it wasn't uncommon for half Elv children to get their swirls in their early teen years.

When the boys reached running age at eighteen months, they became terrors, constantly escaping from minders. Most of the castle staff took to carrying sweets in their pockets as bribes.

Lukas's grief was insurmountable in the beginning. Iris stayed with Lukas for a while, and between her and his parents, they pulled him out of the pit he'd fallen into. Kamron didn't know how to talk to him at first. As if his loss was a wall between them. Iris made Lukas take trips with her every other week to Tate so he could see his son, and they were always hard meetings. Gabe looked so much like his mother. It was difficult for Lukas to see Gabe as anything other than a reminder of his loss, and so Gabe stayed in Tate while Lukas and Iris returned to Arnav after each trip.

Gabe didn't mind, and neither did Keth. The two boys were easygoing as long as they were together. When they were separated, put in different beds, or made to bathe separately, they threw tempers, stomped their little feet, and screamed loud enough to burst an eardrum. Then there was Gabe's uncanny ability to disappear in a room full of adults. Kamron was sure it must be magic, even if he didn't sense any, but Siblina blamed Keth, saying he always made a distraction of some sort right before they lost Gabe. He was never gone for long, and usually returned with sweets he shared with Keth.

Kamron thought it was adorable, and Siblina said it was a problem for another day.

The boy's second birthdays came, and they had a joint party in Arnav. Family and friends gathered in the great hall and ate cake while the toddlers ran about and smeared frosting covered fingers into the hems of the guests' fine clothing.

"We can't separate the boys," Iris said, when the topic of Gabe staying in Arnav came up.

"What if we treat it like an exchange?" Siblina suggested.

"You mean like we take them for a month, then they take them for a month?" Kamron asked.

"That could work," Iris said and turned to Lukas. "What do you think?"

Lukas looked up at the others, as if only just noticing they were standing there. He glanced at Iris, then away, his cheeks redlining. "Yes, I agree."

"Keth, no!" Siblina said, and snatched the boy as he pulled on the tablecloth, inching the large cake closer to the edge.

Iris snorted and poked the baby in the nose. "Now that would have been a mess to remember."

Siblina's eyes got big. "Could you imagine? They'd be scraping up frosting for ages."

"You'd think with so many adults in the room, the kids wouldn't get up to so much trouble." Kamron looked around. "Where's Gabe?"

Kamron turned, expecting to see him wiping his frosting covered fingers on the king's pant leg, but he was gone. A polished shoe stuck out from under a tablecloth. Lifting up the edge of the cloth revealed a very happy Gabe holding out a piece of cake to one of the palace cats, who purred furiously as it licked off the frosting.

"No! Kitty!" Gabe yelled, dropping his cake as Iris picked him up.

Iris made a face. "Woo. Let's go find some sucker to change your diaper."

Siblina laughed and left with her to get Keth changed, and Kamron put an arm over Lukas's shoulder.

"How are you doing?" Kamron asked.

Lukas seemed so distracted, but his face tightened and his cheeks flushed. "I think I messed up."

Kamron led him to one of the food tables, further from the guests. "Well, it's good you have me and we can fix anything. What happened?"

Lukas grimaced. "Iris and I kissed last night."

"Oh. Is that it?" Kamron asked.

"What do you mean 'is that it'? It's huge! I've betrayed Briony. I kissed another woman, and she's barely been gone a year."

Lukas looked away and Kamron didn't want him to slip into his emotions, which were always so close. Kamron shrugged. "I kind of thought you two were already together."

"What? No. I mean, last night . . . But that was sort of a surprise . . ." Lukas's frown deepened.

"Lukas, you have nothing to apologize for. Iris is great, and she's always had a thing for you."

"She has?" A look of wonder crossed his face, and Kamron bit his lip, not sure if he should have said anything.

"I mean, I always thought you kind of liked her too."

"I did." Lukas turned and found her in the crowd. "I don't think I would have survived this last year without her."

"I'm sorry I wasn't there for you."

"You were," Lukas said, looking up at his best friend. "You took care of Gabe, and I can never repay that debt."

"It's not a debt. It's been wonderful, really. Like having twins. You'll see when you keep them for the next month, while Siblina and I take a vacation."

Lukas laughed, and it sounded a little hoarse, like he hadn't done it for a while. "You deserve it."

"I'll remind you that you said that when you return them in a month." They turned back to the party, but a glow in Kamron's pocket caught his eye. He pulled out the communication orb. "I'll be right back," he told Lukas. Ducking into an empty hall, he answered the orb. Rightwitch's face appeared, and Kamron was instantly on edge. "Commander. How are things?"

"Sir Kamron. Olive and Dann have been missing for the last twelve hours. Searches have returned no trace of them."

"They were scouting together?"

"Yes. Since Rian's disappearance, no one has left our camp alone."

Kamron frowned. He hadn't told Rightwitch that Rian had been found, and the news of his arrival and the magic surrounding him was kept quiet. "What was their last known location?"

"To the south of the bat ridge. We've continued searching for additional exits from the cave and, based on gravel patterns, believe we are getting close."

"You told them not to engage?" Kamron asked.

"Yes."

Kamron blew out a breath. "Do you need reinforcements?" With three losses, Rightwitch was down to a team of five. It would make splitting shifts harder.

"No. I have two more coming in the spring. Dann was looking to change positions, and the other was to replace Rian."

"If Dann was looking to leave, do you think there's a chance he deserted?"

Rightwitch frowned. "Anything is possible, but I wouldn't believe it."

Kamron nodded. "Keep me posted."

He signed off and put the orb back in his pocket. With any luck, the two missing soldiers were off canoodling and would not turn up dancing anywhere. Kamron returned to the party and tried to act as if the world wasn't falling down around him.

Five months later, Kamron joined his father for a council meeting. They were in a heated discussion about taxes on specific industries, and Kamron desperately wished he could leave. Lukas and Iris left with the boys only an hour before, and Siblina was somewhere in the castle waiting for Kamron to be done with work so they could relax and pick up where they'd left off in a book they were reading together.

The door to the council room opened, and two soldiers in dirty Alunan uniforms walked in.

"Can we help you?" a clerk asked, standing by the door.

Dann and Olive, Rightwitch's lost soldiers, turned to King Silas on the other side of the table and bowed. They reached for knives in their belts, and everyone in the room jumped into action, but too late. The two soldiers stabbed themselves in the thigh. The entire room stilled as the soldiers pulled the knives out and stabbed themselves again.

"Stop them," Silas called, and Kamron leapt forward. He tried to wrestle the knife from Olive, but the woman evaded him, desperate to continue stabbing herself.

Kamron grabbed her wrist and was able to hold it off her leg with both hands, then his father came around and pulled the knife from her hand. Olive went ballistic, but they pinned her with the help of two lords and a lady, while others tried to get the knife from Dann.

"Marc, call for the guards and track down my wife," Silas ordered to a wide-eyed clerk. "Tell her we need potions for two more."

It took the guards five minutes to subdue Olive, and Elodie seven minutes to reach the council rooms with the potion they'd used on Rian. The healers carried out the wounded.

Silas turned to Kamron. "Call Rightwitch north. Call north any of our people south of the Variant Forest. I don't care about bandits. Keep our uniformed people away from the mountains."

Kamron nodded. He called home any patrols in the south. Then he called Rightwitch and told him to lie low and observe from afar, but to not abandon post.

# Chapter Fifteen

*And when something ends, there is always a new beginning. For better or for worse.*

*Far away from the castle of Tate, high in the mountains above the Avi homes, there lived a man, self-isolated from the world. He preferred his isolation, thankful no one could see the shame his life had become without his magic. Oh, he could still do little things, like light a fire or set a trap for nosy soldier spies, but he was a shadow of the man he'd been in his youth, before his foolish attempt at revenge sapped him of his magical strength.*

*His magic had been held captive, along with his victims, for well over a century. But while the victims found a way to escape, his magic had not, and he remained old and crippled, missing most of who he was, until that night.*

*Across the country, in a castle made capital, an old king and his queen sat down for their evening tea in their magical garden fortress. The day had been long and exciting, celebrating their grandson's fourth birthday, and now they were ready for peace and quiet. The king turned to watch a firefly while his wife raised her tea to her nose, but then it was as if millions of fireflies rose around the queen, and the king turned back as the teacup slipped from her fingers. Grim realization hit him as he knew what was coming. He lunged for his wife, determined to hold on tight and not let go, but his fingers met only empty air as he landed on the soft clover, his wife forever pulled out of reach.*

*With the queen's disappearance from their world, an old pact finally completed, and the remnants of the Spell of the Misplaced, as it was known, finally dissolved. Like a rubber band snapping back into itself, the wizard's magic returned with a sharp and sudden crack, waking him from sleep. His skin buzzed with the force of his magic, and he sat up in bed. He ran a hand over each arm, the magic dancing in celebration across his skin. Moving to a shelf, he dug around for an old rusted looking glass. He watched his face as he willed the age to melt away and the man he'd once been before his mistakes return.*

*His heart raced, and he stepped out of his cave to stand in the evening air. It was as if the world had been made new before him, and he wasn't going to sit on the sidelines and watch it pass by this time.*

Kamron woke as Siblina cried out.

"Love, wake up, it's just a dream," Kamron said, reaching out and pulling her against him, still half asleep.

It was the morning after Keth's fourth birthday, and they celebrated late. Kamron wanted nothing more than to sleep in, but Siblina's nightmares, which only plagued her the nine months she'd been pregnant with Keth, were now back in full force.

Siblina jerked awake, and he held her tight as she cried.

"Shhh. It's okay, love. It's just a dream. Everything is fine," he said, wishing he could believe his own words. With Keth her dreams had made her sick, now they made her cry, and a hopeless, terrified look entered her eyes. "We're all going to be okay, baby."

But she shook her head and cried harder.

When her sobs at last came to an end, Kamron rose and drew

his wife a hot bath. The morning light shone through the windows. Kamron hoped his mother would be up. She made a wreath out of some herbs for Siblina last time pregnancy brought on bad dreams, and Siblina said it dulled their intensity, making it easier to sleep.

Once Siblina was steeping, Kamron left his rooms and headed downstairs to his parents' sanctuary. Kamron knocked lightly and slipped into the sitting room. The bedroom door was cracked open, and the garden doors stood open, so his mother must be up. He stepped onto the garden path and spotted his father on the clover clearing. Kamron took his time, hoping the peace of the garden would soothe his nerves, but something wasn't right. When he got closer, he realized his father was still in his clothes from the party, grimy four-year-old fingerprints on his shirt hem, as he sat in the grass, his head hanging.

"Dad. Are you all right?"

A broken teacup lay on the grass near him. "She's gone."

"What?" Kamron looked around. "Where's Mum?"

Silas looked up at his son. His eyes were puffy and red. "She's gone, Kam."

"That's not possible. Did a healer look at her?" Kamron glanced back at their sitting room and the open bedroom door. Was his mother laying there?

"No, Kamron. She's not dead. She's gone. The spell came back for her and took her to her illusion." Silas stood, and he moved slower than Kamron had ever seen him, as if he'd aged a decade in the night.

"That's not possible. The spell was broken decades ago."

Silas shook his head and put a hand on his son's shoulder. "They couldn't break the spell. She made a deal with a god to attach the spell to her life. She freed the others but doomed herself."

Kamron couldn't believe what his father was saying. Maybe the king had a bad dream or hit his head. Kamron's heart raced, and he wanted to check the bedroom, sure his dad must be wrong. "If that were true, she would have told me."

"She told no one but me. The law said she couldn't rule as long as she was under the spell. If anyone found out the spell wasn't really broken, they wouldn't have let her be queen." He squeezed Kamron's shoulder once and trudged back into the sitting room.

Kamron sunk his fingernails into his leg. He felt the sharp pain, so he wasn't dreaming. He followed his father into his bedroom, but the queen wasn't hiding under the blankets.

Something terrible moved down Kamron's spine. "Dad, what was the one thing Mum wanted?" Kamron rubbed at the birthmark on his forearm. He'd always been afraid of how the curse would ruin his life, but he never thought about how it would hurt his mother. He thought only having one child might be it, but now he realized that wouldn't be enough to satiate their curse.

Silas sat on the edge of the bed and carefully took off his cuff links. "She spent the first twenty-five years of her life traveling back and forth between her Earth and our Eres, with no control over when or why. She never decided whether her other world was real or just an illusion, and it prevented her from committing to either life." Silas looked up at his son. "Your mother wanted more than anything to live out her life in only one world, to be able to commit all of herself. Making that pact with the god to bind up her own future meant living the last few decades always knowing one day she would abandon us. It was torture for her."

Kamron shook his head. He had no words. Was this the real reason she waited so long to have him? The reason she never had other children? She couldn't bear to leave them? Kamron's heart was upstairs with Keth, Gabe, and Siblina, who was now likely expecting. He could never bear to leave them.

"If Gedas is still here, tell him we need it to look like she died." Silas spoke slowly as he undressed and climbed into bed. "It's the best way to make sure no one challenges your rule. I'll make the announcement tomorrow that I'm stepping down. I never wanted to be king without your mum." Silas lay his head on his pillow and closed his eyes. "We can hold your coronation in a few weeks. Ask Iris to help plan."

Kamron stormed out of the bedroom and to the mage quarters, where Gedas occupied a guest wing. He wasn't sure how long he pounded on the door before the old wizard opened, an annoyed expression on his brow.

"Did you know?" Kamron asked, pushing his way into the room.

"Know that you're an annoying boy? Yes, but it seemed improper to point it out."

"Did you know my mother didn't break the spell of the Misplaced? That she tied it to her own life and freed everyone else?"

Gedas's eyebrows went up, and he got a faraway look on his face. "Oh, my stupid little Gull." Gedas sighed, and a look flashed in his eyes that on anyone else Kamron would call regret.

"Can we get her back?"

Gedas shook his head, and Kamron slammed his fist against a bookcase.

"That's not good enough. We need to do something."

The old wizard truly looked old for a moment. He let out a withered sigh. "Where's your father?"

"He's sleeping. He asked if you could help fake her death."

Gedas nodded. "I will do what I can." The wizard left him standing there.

Kamron shook his head, unable to believe what was happening, but unable to see any other option. He returned to his rooms.

Siblina still soaked in their big tub. Kamron slipped off his shoes and climbed into the tub, clothes and all.

"What's wrong?" she asked.

Kamron told her and cried. "I'm not ready to be king."

Siblina sighed and sank into the water. "I have a feeling that's one of those things no one is ever ready for."

Kamron shook his head, at a loss for words. He couldn't imagine a world without his mother.

"I think we should send the boys to Arnav for a few months," Siblina said, and her eyes were worried.

"Okay," Kamron agreed, not about to argue with anything Siblina suggested. She wouldn't tell him if it was a warning from her dreams, so he would trust her. "Keth and Gabe like playing with the babies. We'll send all the nursemaids to help." Iris and Lukas were married in a small ceremony almost two years before, and Iris gave birth to twin boys a year later. She was pregnant again, but they would understand when Kamron asked them to keep the boys for a while. "Should you maybe go with them?" Kamron asked.

Siblina shook her head. "I'm staying with you."

"I worry about you and the baby." Siblina hadn't seen a healer yet to confirm, but they both knew she was pregnant.

"We will go when the time comes," Siblina said, and the "when" broke Kamron's heart.

"You already know it will come to you leaving," Kamron said, his heart shattering into a thousand little pieces.

She didn't reply but placed one hand on her stomach protectively.

"If you know, then why wait? Why tempt the fates?" he asked.

Siblina shook her head. "I belong with you."

That night, as word spread and the nation mourned the death of their queen, Kamron orbed Rightwitch. "The wizard needs to be ended."

"Sir?" Rightwitch asked.

"The wizard is a critical threat to Aluna. You and your team need to end him tonight."

Rightwitch nodded. "Yes, Your Majesty."

# Chapter Sixteen

"Desert your post and you will be tried for your crimes," Kamron growled into the orb.

"I'm not deserting, I'm fleeing for my life," Henri, one of Rightwitch's soldiers said, through gasping breaths as he ran along a mountain path. Kamron could see nothing but twilight sky and gray stone surrounding the soldier.

"Stop. soldier, calm down and tell me what happened. Where is Rightwitch?"

"I told you. He's gone." He stopped long enough to catch his breath. "The six of us went into the cave, I was the rear guard. The others were caught in some spell. Rightwitch got the orb to me, and I ran."

"Did you see the wizard?"

"No, I'm still alive, remember?" Henri said. He set down the globe and Kamron got a full view as the soldier packed a bag.

Kamron peeked out of his dressing room, but Siblina was still in the bath. He closed the door and hissed into the orb.

"Soldier, I as your king command you to go back into that cave. If the others aren't dead, we still have a chance to salvage this. The wizard must be killed."

"All due respect, Your Majesty. I'm not dying for you. I reported in as a last favor to Rightwitch. I've done that, and you can go suck an egg for all I care."

The orb went dead and Kamron cursed. Being king sucked, and he'd only been doing it four months. He couldn't even get his dad to clean up his messes now.

Unraveling. Everything was unraveling. That was Kamron's power, wasn't it? He could unravel magic all day long, but building? Creating? Strengthening? What hope did his future have if he could only destroy?

# Chapter Seventeen

"You need to wake up," Siblina said in Kamron's ear, one clammy palm stroking his forehead, as if she'd been at it a while.

"What? Is the baby here?" Kamron said groggily. It was too early, he needed to fetch a healer.

But Siblina ran a hand over his shoulder. "No, my love, but something is happening."

Kamron didn't question it. He rose and pulled on yesterday's clothes, just getting in his tunic when someone pounded on the door.

"Your Majesty, open up! I have urgent news."

Kamron opened the door to a red-faced commander, four armored soldiers behind him. "What's happened, Joon?"

"The capital has been infiltrated. The castle is surrounded," Commander Joon said through heavy gasps.

Kamron blinked and spun into motion, reaching for the orb on the nightstand. "Tell our forces at the border to head north and support the capital. We won't let Oskela fall." He focused a thought on Commander Leon at the northern border and the globe started the connection, pulsing as it waited for the man to pick up.

Commander Joon didn't move to deliver Kamron's orders, and so the king looked at the commander. "What is it Joon?"

"No—not the capital of Oskela, Your Majesty. I mean here. Tate has been infiltrated. The castle is surrounded by some force field we can't get past."

It took him a moment to understand, and then the blood drained from Kamron's face. He ducked into the dressing room where he found Siblina, several steps ahead of him. He nodded grimly. "Wrap up tight and wear thick breeches. You need to get out of the city." She nodded once, and he grabbed his boots and sword belt before returning to Joon. "Why did it take this long for word to come?"

Joon shook his head. "We can't get word from outside. The sentries on the castle wall noticed the commotion and sent someone to check, then discovered the force field."

"Do we know what's out there?" Kamron asked as he laced his boots. No one said anything, but one soldier shifted on her feet. Kamron pointed at her. "You, what did you see?"

She shook her head, her face flushed and full of terror. "I was on the wall, watching the fighting, sir. They seem crazed, sir. They don't respond to words, and they keep fighting long after their injuries would drop a normal soldier."

Kamron nodded, the bottom falling out of his stomach. "We need to get the queen out of the castle."

"But sir, wouldn't it be better to hole up in a safe space until it's over?"

The king shook his head. "She needs to get to Rohap."

They didn't question him. Kamron led Siblina downstairs, surrounded by their small guard as others ran through the halls and orders were yelled as the castle woke to the chaos. On the first floor, Silas met them, dressed in basic armor, his sword at his side.

"The garden is the safest place in the castle," Silas said.

Kamron shook his head. "Siblina needs to get out of the city."

"Why?" Silas asked. He didn't disagree or fight Kamron, only checked to make sure his decision-making was sound.

"Because my magic said it's the right plan," Siblina said, and Silas nodded.

"Good enough for me."

They moved down the corridor toward the south entrance, close to the stables, but soldiers came rushing in from the kitchens as they passed. "They've breached the castle!"

Kamron saw the empty-faced fighter as he came up behind the soldier and swung an axe. The soldier went down and Kamron deflected the blow. More guards rushed in to fill the space and Kamron rushed Siblina down the hall. More empty-faced people flooded the kitchen, overwhelming the guards. They looked like farmers and everyday people, carrying any kind of weapon.

As they raced down the hall, guards peeled off their group to defend and deflect, Kamron and Silas beating away the few enemies who snuck through. At the door to the courtyard, Kamron checked for bodies and found none. Slowly he opened the door, and when the coast was clear, they ran for the stables.

A glowing miasma circled the castle, cutting through some of the outlying buildings as if someone placed a bowl over the castle, and sliced through anything in the way. Two-thirds of the stables were cut off to them, but it was enough. They barricaded themselves inside, and Siblina found a horse.

"I'll saddle while you work on the wards," Silas said. Kamron nodded and moved to the glowing force cutting through the stables.

The spell was complex, but not anything he hadn't seen before. He explored it with his magic, looking for its weaknesses. The issue was the power in a ward this size. If he broke it wrong, the backlash would knock them all out. The sounds of battle rang out behind him and Kamron glanced over his shoulder. They'd been discovered.

Silas stood, one shoulder against the door, the other guards fallen around him while Siblina sat in the saddle, ready to flee.

Kamron made eye contact with his father, struggling against the door. "I'll hold the door. You get her out," his father said.

Kamron nodded.

Silas opened the door and slashed an opening, before stepping out and closing the door behind him.

Kamron turned back to the spell, tears falling from his eyes. He had to focus.

He had to make a way for Siblina to escape. So maybe he didn't need to break the force field. Could he lift it? Make an exit just for her that didn't draw any attention?

Kamron wove the spell into the frame of the stables, and then when it was secure, he popped the section of the spell blocking Siblina's retreat.

He laughed and turned to his wife. "It's open. Go."

She urged her horse forward but stopped, tears running down her face. "I can't. I can't leave you."

"I love you. Save our baby."

She leaned down, and he kissed her. The door behind them crashed open, and Siblina urged her horse forward.

"Go!" Kamron yelled and hit the horse's butt. Siblina took off down the narrow path, and Kamron pulled his sword from his belt. Empty-faced fighters moved toward him in a horde, Commander Rightwitch pale and absentmindedly leading the way. They were too pressed in to make much use of their weapons, and Kamron swung his sword, cutting down innocent people. As bodies fell, he stepped further and further back, but he held the line. The longer he fought, the more time Siblina had to escape. Kamron wasn't sure how long he lasted, his feet sliding on the wet floorboards, when the empty-faced horde stopped.

Kamron paused. His chest heaved and his left hand flew to the bleeding slash on his right arm. Was that it? Would Siblina get through without notice?

A man poked his head into the stables and made a face at the mess. He looked like Gedas but twenty years younger. The man looked up at Kamron and grinned, and he no longer looked like the wizard he'd known his whole life. This man had a gleam of excitement in his eye as he stepped over the fallen fighters toward Kamron.

The man flicked his hand, and a spell hit Kamron, freezing his arms and legs. Kamron's heart raced. He'd never seen someone cast magic so effortlessly. He took a few calming breaths and then picked apart the spell. It was complex, and that worried Kamron. Once free, he raised his sword.

"Ooh. That's a nice trick." The man flicked another spell, and Kamron broke it faster this time.

"Who are you?" Kamron asked.

"What? Your mother didn't tell you about me?" the man said, as he stepped over another person. His voice was light and playful, and it set Kamron's teeth on edge. "She said she would, you know. She said her and her own would leave me be, leave me in peace. Then YOU tried to *kill* me?" The man screeched out the words and it took all Kamron's will not to flinch.

Kamron shook his head, not wanting to believe who this man could be. A wraith straight from his mother's stories, and her warnings. The one rule she told him never to disobey. "They said you were old and weak, your power tied up in your own madness," Kamron said.

The man straightened and tapped his chin, a calm quizzical expression on his face, as if he'd been asked an interesting question and not just invaded a castle.

"That was true once. The spell that trapped your mother trapped me as well, but then it became complete." Wizard Viclor grinned.

He tossed another spell at Kamron, and the king didn't even let it form before he unraveled it. The wizard tossed another and another, and another, and Kamron panted as he broke them.

"That's a real nice trick you have," Viclor said again. "But what if we do this?"

He flicked another spell, and this one stuck itself to Kamron like glue, and when it connected, pain radiated up his body and he fell to the ground, frozen in place. His body was on fire with blue magic, and he couldn't think, couldn't focus on the magic to unwind it.

Viclor giggled and closed the distance between them. He bent down, glee clear on his face until he was inches from Kamron's nose.

"That's what I was missing, what I didn't realize," Viclor said, his voice quiet and quick. "She said they broke the spell, the sneaky chit. She didn't tell me the god tied the spell to her and her alone. Such self-sacrifice, a noble ending, but she didn't tell ME."

The pain lessened, and Kamron could think again, but when he examined the spell holding him tight, he couldn't find an end to unravel.

Kamron remembered his mother's stories of this man. They ran through his mind often over the years as the fear of him guided Kamron's actions. Decades ago, the wizard was a rambling mess, unable to communicate his thoughts in a way anyone could follow, but that wasn't who now stood over him. This man was clearly unhinged, but he was clear and coherent, and deadly.

"Would it have made a difference, had you known?" Kamron asked.

Viclor straightened and paced in a small circle, dancing over fallen fighters, before turning back. "No. I suppose it doesn't make a difference, but it shows her character. She was a liar. She vowed she and hers would leave me alone. That's all I asked. Just to be left alone, but then you betrayed that, and you are hers, so she lied and broke her vow."

The spell tightened around Kamron until it became hard to breathe. He coughed, but air refused to rush back into his lungs.

Viclor leaned down once again. "Don't worry. I will keep your kingdom safe in your absence. I can make it better than it was. Trust me, I don't lie like she did."

Kamron's mind slowed, drifting calmly, separate from his body.

He'd tried so hard not to want anything in his life. He failed in the end and wanted to grow old with Siblina. Then he wanted a family, to see Keth and any other children grow up and have children of their own. He'd wanted it with all his heart, and after wanting nothing for so long, it must have been too much temptation for the curse of his family.

But that was okay.

If he could not be there and be with them, at least they would have a chance of a future without him.

Two months later, in a small village often forgotten, just as a queen took her last breath, another life entered the world, and she went unseen.

## The story of the Twoshy continues...

Sibley has lived her life trying to be invisible until a tragedy drives her from her home into the protection of a forest where she discovers several unlikely friends who hold the keys to her past and her future. Join her as she finds her path in A Girl Unseen, coming 2023.

For exclusive content, pronunciation guides, short stories, and a guide to the Twoshy, visit our website:

www.authorheathermichelle.com

Instagram: @heathermichely

Tiktok: @AuthorHeatherMichelle

# About the Author

Heather Michelle is an emerging author of young adult fantasy. She lives in Acworth, GA with her cats; Fitzwilliam, and Mister Bingley, and a slew of unique roommates.

Growing up, Heather Michelle spent more time living in her imagination than outside of it. Small town life sandwiched between the redwood forests and the Pacific ocean provided a rich scope for the imagination. Before the age of twelve, Heather Michelle was not a reader, but a chance encounter with a rented audiobook launched her into the vast world of the printed word, and she never looked back.

www.ingramcontent.com/pod-product-compliance
Lightning Source LLC
Chambersburg PA
CBHW030531310726
48979CB00010B/1876/J
* 9 7 8 1 9 5 2 8 5 7 1 4 0 *